MW00743963

Flicker

ROB H HUNT

Copyright © 2014 by Rob H Hunt

ISBN 978-1-312-38981-6

All rights reserved. This book or any portion thereof may not be reproduced or used in any manner whatsoever without the express written permission of the author except for the use of brief quotations in a book review or scholarly journal.

Published by Rob H Hunt

Printed in the United States of America.

The characters and events in this book are fictitious. Any similarity to real persons, living or dead, is coincidental and not intended by the author.

First Edition

Acknowledgements

I would like to thank my wife Kelly for encouraging me to publish this book, and my three children – Sebastian, Xander and Ryland - for constantly stimulating my imagination.

A special thanks to Ben, Eli, Josh and Lainey for reading an early draft and providing invaluable feedback.

Thanks also to Tanya for listening to my never-ending monologues about characters, plotlines and dialogue.

And finally, a huge thank you to Francine for the hours she spent editing and improving this book.

Flicker would never have been published without any of these fine people and I am eternally indebted to them.

CHAPTER ONE

In a cool, dark, cavernous room, something was very wrong.

CHAPTER TWO

The clock radio sprung to life at 8:30 am. Joel lay in bed for a few minutes listening to a static-filled rendition of a classic rock song that he would never usually tolerate but was too tired to turn off. When he couldn't take it anymore, he reached out and whacked the bright red digital clock that sat on the table by his bed. The music came to an abrupt stop and Joel lay for a few more moments enjoying the silence.

With a heavy sigh, he sat up. He swung his legs over the side of the bed, planted his feet on the floor and rubbed his eyes. Then Joel remembered – it was Saturday! No school and no responsibilities, unless you consider soccer practice a responsibility, which Joel definitely did not.

He looked around his room for something to wear. He didn't have a big bedroom – there was barely room for his bed, and the chest of drawers. One wall was lined with shelves that were packed with books, toys, collectables and other treasures. The small amount of floor space that he did have was covered by a bright red carpet with a large smiley face. He grabbed a pair of shorts and a T-shirt, got dressed and headed downstairs.

The house was completely silent, which was unusual - Joel had a younger brother, Marc, who could be counted on to cause a general uproar wherever he was. There was no sign of his parents either. It wasn't completely unheard of for his mom and dad to have gone somewhere without him, but usually they told him about it beforehand.

Joel walked into the kitchen and opened the fridge. He was not exactly sure what he would find there, but he was in no way prepared for the sight that met his eyes. The fridge was empty. Totally empty. There was no food, no shelves, no light, and no color: just dark emptiness. It was like a black hole had materialized inside the refrigerator.

Joel slammed the door closed and waited for a few seconds. The palm of his hand felt clammy against the door handle and he shivered.

He swallowed hard, and then opened the fridge for a second time. Everything looked totally normal: there was milk, juice, a couple of yogurts, some cheese and a produce drawer filled with a variety of green stuff.

"OK," he muttered to himself. "Weird."

He put a hand on his forehead, but didn't seem to be warmer than usual. He had definitely lost his interest in food, however, and closed the fridge door.

He looked around the kitchen, but everything else seemed normal. There were a couple of dirty dishes by the sink, the kettle was sitting on the island in the middle of the kitchen, and the table near the fireplace was empty except for a small pile of mail.

He wondered where his family had gone. He couldn't remember his mom or dad saying they would be leaving early that morning, but then again he didn't always pay attention when they were talking to him.

Joel slipped on a pair of gray sneakers that he had left next to the kitchen door the night before and walked out into the warming morning air. It was another perfect day – sunny with just a few clouds lazily traversing the sky. He walked across the yard and up the shared driveway that connected his house and two neighboring houses with the street.

Soccer practice would start in about 30 minutes and it was going to take Joel that long to get there if he had to walk. It really was pretty rude of his parents to leave him without a ride. Still, in another few years he would be driving himself.

He walked up the tree-lined street and took a right turn towards the town center. There were no sidewalks where he lived, but it was a quiet area and there were few cars on the road. The houses along the street were all of a similar style – large, red brick buildings with a double garage to the side. They all had expansive front yards, some with swing sets or trampolines, but Joel didn't see anyone playing outside as he passed by.

He made his way down the winding road, thinking about soccer. Coach had him playing center back, but he really wanted to move into a midfield position. It wasn't that he was bad in defense, but he felt that midfield would make better use of his sprinting and passing skills. Plus, he was pretty small for a defender – only 5' 1" – and that definitely made his job tougher. Not that he was complaining, Joel was not a complainer, and he was happy to be on the team. He just wanted a change of pace.

He reached the end of the street and took another right. This was a much busier road as it was the main North/South thoroughfare that connected several nearby towns. Luckily the street had been upgraded a couple of years ago, and there was a sidewalk for pedestrians. As the cars zipped past, Joel's mind roamed from one subject to another: school, soccer, his absent parents... and Cassandra.

He sighed deeply. Cassandra... Just the thought of her made his heart race. It wasn't just that she was pretty – which she was – but she was also smart, funny and loved soccer. In other words, she was perfect. Unfortunately, Joel was pretty sure that Cassandra did not feel the same way about him. Sure, she would smile when she saw him at school, but she smiled at everyone – that was just the sort of person that she was. And yes, she did say "Hi" to him when they had Spanish class together, but again, this was just her being friendly. That was another thing he liked about her. She was so nice.

Joel reached the entrance to North End Park and jogged up the path. The soccer fields were at the far end of the park, past the lake and the baseball diamonds. He noticed several people fishing in the lake, staring intently into the water. Now that was an activity that he just didn't get – talk about boring! As far as Joel was concerned, you might as well spend your time watching grass grow. It offered the same level of excitement, without having to impale slimy worms on a barbed hook. Ugh.

Soccer practice was just starting. The rest of the team were running laps, calling out to each other and laughing. Joel picked up his pace and ran over to where Coach was studying a clipboard.

"Sorry I'm late," he said. "My mom and dad totally flaked out on me. I had to walk the whole way."

Coach gave him a strange look. "What?"

"My parents were supposed to give me a ride to practice, but they were already gone when I woke up."

"And you are...?" said Coach

Joel looked around nervously. Coach was not known for his sense of humor. In fact, Joel was not sure if he ever saw him smile except when his team scored.

"Your name?" repeated Coach.

Joel decided to play along. "I'm Joel," he said, "your favorite defense superstar."

Coach did not look amused. "Are you trying to be funny?" he scowled.

9

"No. I thought you were," said Joel.

"Obviously you don't know me kid, but I am not funny."

"Then why are you pretending you don't know me?" asked Joel. "Is it just because I am late?"

Coach bent down to stare directly into Joel's eyes. "I'm not sure who you are or what you're up to, but you better turn around and walk away right now."

Joel took a step back. He had never seen Coach act this way before and it unnerved him. He glanced over at the rest of the team. They had stopped running and were all looking in his direction. Joel took another step back from Coach, then turned and ran towards the group of boys.

"Hey guys!" he yelled as he ran. "What did I miss?"

His teammates did not reply, but continued to stare at him as he approached.

Joel slowed to a walk and then stopped altogether. "Hey Alex," he called to one of his friends on the team. "How was karate yesterday?" Alex was one of the most athletic boys that Joel knew. Not only was he the top scorer on the team, he was also one step away from being a black belt at karate.

Alex took a step towards Joel and then stopped. He shook his head quickly, as if trying to rid himself of an annoying fly. "You..." he began, but trailed off into silence. He stared at Joel for a moment. "How do you know my name?" he asked.

Before Joel could reply, Coach was back and in his face.

"Listen to me." Coach was speaking more slowly than usual and his voice was deeper and more gravely, almost like a growl. "I am going to count to three, and if you are not gone by the time I finish, I am going to personally remove you. You do not belong here." He paused for a moment.

"One..."

Joel gulped and glanced over at his teammates again. Nobody was smiling.

"Two..."

This was crazy. He had been on this team for three months now, and he knew every single one of these guys.

"Th–"

Joel turned and ran.

CHAPTER THREE

Joel didn't stop running until he reached the lake. Panting, he flopped down on the grass, and tried to figure out what was going on. He couldn't understand what he had done to make Coach and his team behave so crazily.

He thought back to last Wednesday's game. He had played well, perhaps even better than usual, and his team had won a decisive victory. True, he had conceded a penalty in the last ten minutes of the game (it really wasn't his fault — the other player had taken a dive and fooled the ref), but it didn't make any difference to the outcome. Surely this couldn't be the reason why Coach and the team were treating him like this.

He looked over to where the practice was taking place. The boys had resumed running laps, and Coach was watching them intently, barking instructions every now and then. Nobody was paying any attention to him.

"Fine," thought Joel. "If they want to act like jerks, who needs them?" He got up and decided to stop by *FroYo's Frozen Yogurt Emporium* before heading home. He definitely deserved a treat today.

FroYo's was on the edge of the town center just over the bridge that crossed the train tracks. It took less than five minutes to reach the store from the park, and Joel spent most of that time pondering the strange behavior of Coach and his teammates. It just didn't add up. He began to wonder if it had been a huge prank and he had overreacted.

FroYo's was one of three stores in a short strip mall: on one side there was a sports equipment shop, and on the other side a pizza restaurant — *Mario's Pizzeria*. Joel loved *Mario's* — they let you make your own pizza with whatever toppings you wanted, and then they cooked it for you. His all-time favorite was the Pepperoni, Peppers and

Peanut pizza that he had invented (he called it *The Three Ps*), but this morning, he was focused on frozen yogurt.

Nothing soothed the soul and eased the mind like a cup of *FroYo's* with six toppings. Feeling better already, Joel walked into the store. There was no line – the day was rapidly improving – and he walked directly up to the server who was standing behind the counter. "I'll have a FroYo Six to stay."

The server smiled. "Sure thing. That will be five dollars, please."

Joel handed her his card and waited while she swiped it at the register. A frown crossed her face, and she swiped the card again. The register beeped rapidly. The server looked confused. She examined the card closely for a moment and then turned her attention back to Joel.

"I'm sorry," she said, "but the charge is not authorized."

"What do you mean?" asked Joel.

She smiled again. "I mean, you cannot use the card to purchase anything. It is not authorized. In fact, I am not even allowed to give it back to you."

"You can't keep it!" cried Joel. "It's mine! Besides, I need it to buy stuff."

"I'm sorry," said the server, still smiling, "but you will not be able to buy anything with this card ever again. It is not authorized. I'm going to destroy it now." With that, she slid the card into a small slot at the side of the register. There was an unpleasant grinding sound and then silence. She had shredded it.

"What are you DOING?" yelled Joel. "That's mine! You can't do that!"

The server didn't even flinch. "I'm sorry," she repeated, "but your card was unauthorized. You should leave now."

Joel stared at her in disbelief. She was still smiling at him as if everything was just fine, as if shredding someone's card was a perfectly normal occurrence and not even slightly disturbing.

"You should leave now," she repeated. "Next, please!"

Joel looked over his shoulder and saw that there were two people waiting in line behind him. He was mortified - they must have seen the whole thing. Luckily he didn't think he knew them.

"Don't worry," said the man immediately behind him. "I'm sure it's just a glitch or something. I'll bet you can sort it out when you get home."

Joel was grateful for the stranger's kind words. "Thanks," he said. "You're probably right."

He turned back to the server, but she was ignoring him now. "Can I help you sir?" she said to the man standing behind Joel.

Clearly the conversation was over, and Joel shuffled out of the store. "Worst day ever," he muttered, "by a million miles." For a moment, he considered going back to soccer practice to see if the prank was over, but he decided against it. The way things were going this morning, Coach would probably use him as the ball.

He walked home slowly, hands in his pockets, staring at the ground. Every now and then he would mutter something under his breath. "Ridiculous." "Who cares?" "Stupid." "Whatever."

Eventually he found himself back on his street. As he neared his house, Mrs. Glick, his next door neighbor, drove out of their shared driveway. He waved at her as she passed by, but she didn't even smile in return. She just totally ignored him. "Perfect. Just perfect," he said to nobody in particular.

Joel walked down the driveway and saw his mom's car parked in front of the garage. He wondered how his parents would react to what happened at *FroYo's*. Knowing his luck, they would think he had lost his card and made up the whole story so he wouldn't get in trouble.

The garage door was closed, so Joel walked up the steps to the bright red front door. He turned the handle, but it was locked.

"You're kidding me!" he cried. The front door was never locked! Never, ever. But today, of course, it was locked. He rang the doorbell and waited. A few seconds later, his mom opened the door.

"You would not believe the day I am having," he said as he stepped past her into the hallway. "It is unbelievable. And where were you this morning?"

His mom took a step back and gave him a quizzical look. "Who are you?" she asked.

"Don't even start," said Joel, "because today is not the day to be funny. I think I'm going back to bed and starting again."

He took a step towards the stairs, but his mom gripped him on the shoulder. This wasn't a loving, gentle, reassuring gesture that a mom might make, but a firm and slightly uncomfortable grip.

"I said, who are you?" There was something about her voice that alarmed Joel. It was definitely his mom's voice, but something was different. It had an edge to it that he was not used to hearing. For a brief moment, he thought he might burst into tears – something that he had not done for years – but he fought back the urge.

"What's wrong with everyone today?" he cried. "Did everyone wake up this morning and decide to make Joel's life miserable? If they did, it's working really well!"

His mom started to move him back towards the front door. "I don't know who you are or what you want, but you need to leave right now. If you're in trouble, go see the police. We can't help you here."

This was too much for Joel. He shoved his mom aside and sprinted up the stairs. "Really?" he yelled. "You don't know who I am? Perhaps my bedroom will remind you."

"Get down here now or I am calling the police myself!" shouted his mom. "You do not belong here!"

Joel couldn't believe what he was hearing. This was his mom talking. The one person in the whole world who would always be there for him, always take care of him, always love him. And now she was screaming at him to leave.

Joel heard the back door slam. "What's going on in here?" It was his dad.

"Dad!" he yelled, choking back a sob for the second time in sixty seconds. "I'm up here!"

His father strode into the hallway and glanced at his wife who gave him a frightened look. "There's a teenage boy up there," she said, pointing up the stairs.

His father looked at Joel carefully. "OK," he said. "There is no need to be frightened. Just come down and we can talk."

"What's wrong with mom?" asked Joel. "Is she sick or something? She doesn't know who I am."

His dad put one foot on the bottom stair. "Listen," he said. "I don't know what's going on here, but I can tell you are scared. Just come downstairs and we will sort everything out. If you need help, we will find you help. Just come down quietly."

"Dad?" said Joel. "Why are you talking to me like this? It's me – Joel."

His dad took another step up the stairs. "Everything's going to be OK. Just come down and we will sort everything out."

Joel started to shake. "No, no, no," he whispered. He backed away from the stairs and ran down the hall to his bedroom. Except there was no bedroom. There wasn't even a bedroom door. It was as if his room had never existed.

A wave of nausea washed over Joel and it was all he could do to not throw up. He hit the wall with the palm of his hand. "Where is my room?" he screamed. "What have you done with it?"

CHAPTER FOUR

The cool, dark, cavernous room was a hive of activity. The problem had been located.

CHAPTER FIVE

Joel slumped to the ground sobbing. His dad walked over and hoisted him up under his arms. He dragged him back down the hallway and down the stairs as if he were nothing more than a sack of potatoes. Joel didn't even try to resist. He was still shaking, and his sobs were now mixed with hiccups. He felt completely drained and out of touch with his surroundings.

His dad didn't stop when they reached the front door. He dragged him outside, up the driveway, and dumped him by the side of the road.

He stood over Joel, staring down at him. "You don't belong here," he said. "Don't come back." With that, he turned and walked away.

Joel lay on the ground and watched his dad go. He was exhausted, and beyond confused. What was happening to him? Why was everyone treating him like he was a stranger? Where had his bedroom gone? Perhaps he had lost his mind. Maybe everyone else was right and he was wrong. Perhaps he wasn't really Joel, this wasn't his home, and he didn't live in this town. Maybe he had had an accident, and hurt his head, and was hallucinating.

He sat up and wiped the tears from his eyes. This was totally messed up. He knew who he was and he knew where he lived. He wasn't crazy and his head was fine. He just needed to figure out what was going on so that everything could get back to normal. But where to start? Everything was so bewildering that he had no idea what to do. Even worse, if he couldn't rely on his mom and dad, then who could he trust?

Ben. He could trust Ben. Joel had known him forever. Ben was his oldest friend and one of the most laid-back kids he knew. Ben only lived a couple of streets away – Joel could be there in less than five minutes. He picked himself up, wiped his eyes once more, and started back up the street.

It was then that he noticed her for the first time. A girl, probably two or three years older than Joel, was standing at the top of his street staring at him. She seemed unnaturally still, almost as if she had been frozen in place. She had straight dark hair that came down to her shoulders and was wearing a simple blue sleeveless dress that ended below her knees. She looked like she was dressed to go to a fancy restaurant or to a dance. As he got nearer, she turned and walked away.

"Can I help you?" Joel called out.

The girl stopped and looked back at him. She shook her head sadly and then continued to walk away.

There was something about the girl that held his attention. Joel didn't recognize her, but it was like he knew her. She felt significant to him, but he had no idea why. For a moment he thought about following her and finding out who she was and what she was doing, but she was walking in the opposite direction from Ben's house and he was in a hurry.

He walked up the street and took a left. Ben's street ran parallel to his, but there was no shortcut between the houses. They had talked about trying to dig a tunnel that would link their backyards, but it had never gotten beyond the planning stage. Given the fact that the tunnel would have to be about two hundred yards long and would go underneath another street and at least two different homes, this was probably a good thing.

As Joel got closer to his house he started to feel anxious. Yes, Ben was a good friend, probably his best friend, but the events of the morning had shaken Joel to his core, and he still felt mildly nauseous. There was no rational explanation for what had transpired, particularly for his parents' behavior, and he was becoming more and more nervous about what would happen when he saw Ben. He decided to proceed with caution.

Just like Joel, Ben lived in a house that shared a long driveway with two other homes. Ben's was the second of the three, but Joel came to a stop when he reached the first house. He had a clear view of Ben's home from here, but he was partially hidden from view by a tall tree that stood at the top of the neighbor's lawn. There was no visible activity at the house: the front door was closed and the garage was shut. Joel wondered what to do next. He had two clear choices: either he walked up to the house and asked for Ben, or... or what? OK, maybe he only had one choice.

"Hello?" Ben's neighbor must have seen him loitering by the tree and had come out to investigate. "Are you looking for something?"

"Sorry, no." replied Joel. "I'm here to see Ben."

"Oh, ok," said the neighbor. "You know he lives in the next house, right?"

"Right, yes. Thanks!"

"No problem," smiled the neighbor. "Have a good day!"

Joel realized that this was the most normal interaction he had had today. There had been nothing crazy or weird about the conversation – it had been a perfectly unremarkable exchange. He set off towards Ben's house, feeling a little more hopeful.

He walked up to the front door and rang the bell. There was the sound of footsteps coming down the stairs inside the house, and Cassandra opened the door.

Joel felt like he had been punched in the stomach. "Wh...?" he spluttered.

Cassandra smiled. "Are you looking for Ben? Hang on a sec." She turned and looked up the stairs. "Ben!" she yelled, "Are you done? It's for you!"

"Cassandra?" said Joel.

Cassandra turned back and looked at him. "Ummm, yes?" she replied.

"What... I mean... Why are you-"

He was interrupted by Ben bounding down the stairs. "Yo, what's up?"

"Ben," cried Joel, "thank God you recognize me! I was beginning to think I might be going crazy!"

"Er... OK," said Ben.

"Everyone is acting as if they don't know who I am, my bedroom disappeared and my dad threw me out in the street! I need to figure out what's happening to me, and why. And I need your help."

"Look dude," said Ben, "I'm not sure if we met someplace – I'm terrible at remembering people – but I don't think I can help you. Maybe you should go see your mom."

"Stop it!" screamed Joel in a high pitched voice that he barely recognized. "Just stop it now! This isn't funny! I am Joel, and you are my best friend Ben. And this," he pointed at Cassandra, "is Cassandra. And by the way, why is she at your house? You barely know her! Is this all part of the plan to make my head explode?"

"Whoa dude!" said Ben, taking hold of Cassandra's arm and stepping further back into the hall. "Calm down, OK?"

"Calm down?" cried Joel. "You know what? I'll calm down when you and everyone else stop torturing me and admit that you know who I am!"

Cassandra, brave and wonderful Cassandra, released her arm from Ben's grip, took a small step forward and reached out to touch Joel's face. She held her hand against his cheek and stared into his eyes. "I'm sorry," she said after a couple of seconds. "I thought, just for a moment, there was something about you that... but I was wrong." She withdrew her hand and stepped back.

Joel stared at the two of them standing in Ben's hallway. They looked confused and concerned and he realized that this was not some grand game that people were playing. Something had happened to him and now everything was wrong.

He pressed his fingertips into his forehead and took a deep breath. "I'm sorry," he said after a moment. "I didn't mean to scare you. I'll go." He turned and started to walk away.

"Hey dude!" Ben called out, "Good luck, OK?"

Joel didn't bother responding. He walked up the shared driveway and back onto the street. His entire world had fallen apart, but he felt strangely calm. Everything was clear to him now. He had been right before: he must have lost his mind. Everything he thought he knew was wrong. Everyone he thought he knew was a stranger. He must have had a mental breakdown or something, and he obviously needed help.

"Right," he said to himself as he made his way back up the street. "It's all going to be OK. I'll just go to the hospital and they'll figure it out."

It felt good to have a plan, even if the plan was based on his being crazy. The hospital would be able to help him. He would get his memory back and he would go home – wherever that was.

The hospital was on the other side of the town center, and it would take him at least an hour to walk there, but he had a new sense of purpose and felt reenergized. He shoved his hands in his pockets and set off.

CHAPTER SIX

Joel walked at a brisk pace, past his street and down towards the main road. He tried not to think about his situation, no good could come of that, but instead focused on the beautiful day. The sun was higher in the sky now, and it was an ideal temperature – not too hot and not too cold. The leaves on the trees that dotted the front yards he passed were a perfect shade of green and seemed to shimmer in the bright sunshine.

As he neared the bottom of the road, he saw the girl in the blue dress sitting on the ground, leaning against a tree. She was hugging her knees to her chest and gazing into the distance.

Joel had the same uneasy reaction to her presence as before. There was something about this girl – something that mattered – and this time he was going to investigate. He walked over to her and sat down on the grass a few feet to her left.

She made no movement – nothing that would indicate she knew he was there. This was the closest he had been to her, and he took the opportunity to get a better look. Her skin was darker than Joel's, and she had large brown eyes that were set far apart in a pixie-shaped face.

Joel waited for a few moments to see if she would speak, but she remained silent, so he decided to break the ice. "Hi. I'm Joel."

She turned and looked at him, but didn't respond.

"Why are you sitting here?" he asked.

She shrugged her shoulders and turned away again. "Where would you prefer I sit?"

Her voice had an iciness that Joel had not expected.

"No," he said hurriedly, "I didn't mean that. I just meant that this seemed like a strange place to hang out, you know? I mean, you're all dressed up, but sitting on the grass under a tree. It just seems sort of weird."

She gave a short, sharp laugh. "Ha! Weird... that's a good one."

Joel ignored her flippant tone. "Yes - weird. And now I suppose you are going to tell me to get lost."

"Maybe I am."

"Fine," said Joel. "It just goes along with my messed up, sucky day."

"Don't talk to me about *your* messed up day," she sneered. "You don't know what you're talking about."

"Look," said Joel, finally irritated by her attitude. "I have no idea what your deal is, but there is no way you are having a worse or weirder day than me, OK?"

The girl turned back to him. "Really?" she scoffed.

"Yes, really."

"Fine – beat this. Last night, I was on a date with my boyfriend Craig at *Bon Appetit*." Joel had heard of this restaurant – it was a very fancy place where the waiters all spoke in French accents. "Everything was going great. He's funny, I'm funny. He's cute, I look great.

"After we ordered, I go to the bathroom for a couple of minutes. When I come back, he's gone. I mean completely disappeared. And that's not all. Someone else is sitting at our table, so I go over to them and ask what's going on and why they have taken our seats. They look at me like I'm insane. A waiter comes over and says I'm making a scene and have to leave. He tells me I don't belong there.

"Now things started to go really nuts. The waiter says he doesn't remember me or Craig and he doesn't remember taking my order – even though I know he did!" She paused for a moment and shook her head in disbelief.

"So I go outside – there's no sign of Craig and there's no sign of his car. I was mad, I mean really mad. I walk all the way home, which takes me more than an hour – and this is in the dark, by the way. When I get home..." her voice trailed off.

"Let me guess," said Joel. "You parents didn't know you, your house isn't your house anymore, and everyone treats you like a stranger."

The girl looked up and glared at him. "How did you know that?"

She jumped to her feet and stood over him with her eyes blazing and her fists clenched tightly at her sides. "I said, how do you know that?"

Joel stood up quickly and backed away from the girl. She was at least two inches taller than him and for a moment he found her alarmingly intimidating. "The reason I know," he said, "is because the same thing happened to me."

The girl looked confused for a moment. "What do you mean?"

Joel quickly told her about the events of this morning and the conclusion he had reached regarding his mental health.

When he finished, the girl studied him carefully. "What did you say your name was?" she asked.

"Joel."

"I'm Sara," said the girl. She sat back down on the ground. "Did all that stuff really happen to you?"

Joel nodded and sat down facing her.

"And now you think you're crazy?"

"It's the only thing that makes sense," he said.

"Well we can't both be crazy. That's just too much of a coincidence."

Joel thought for a moment. "Perhaps we caught a disease or something. You know, like a brain virus that makes you forget everything and get confused."

Sara nodded slowly. "That's possible," she said, "but how did we both get it? We've never even met before, so we couldn't have got it from each other."

That was a good point, unless.... "What if we actually DO know each other, but have forgotten," said Joel excitedly. "Since the moment I first saw you, I thought you were important, or special in some way, but I have no idea why."

The girl snorted. "You just think I look good in this dress."

"No!" cried Joel. "That's not it at all!"

"Wow, thanks," said Sara sarcastically.

"I mean, yes, you look great, but that's not what I meant. I feel like you matter to me, but I don't know why."

Sara did not respond.

"Do you feel it too?" asked Joel

"There's something... familiar about you," she said finally. "But I don't think you're special or important or anything like that."

Joel shrugged. "Perhaps if I had worn a blue dress..." he said.

Sara smiled briefly. "Perhaps..."

Neither of them spoke for a moment, then Joel got back to his feet. "So," he said, "I'm going to the hospital. Coming?"

Sara shook her head slowly. "I don't know," she said. "I don't feel like I'm crazy. I mean, I'm not hearing voices or seeing monsters or anything like that."

"Me neither," said Joel. "But I don't know who I am or where I live, and I'm betting the hospital can help."

Sara looked up at Joel. "What if it's not us? What if it's everyone else?"

"That's what I thought at first, but I don't see how that makes any sense. They can't all be crazy, it must be us."

Sara stood up and smoothed down her dress. "I'm not sure I agree. And anyway, I don't see why you're so thrilled to have some doctor tell you that you're nuts."

"I'll tell you why," said Joel. "Because then they can fix me and I can go back to my life... back to normal."

"Great," said Sara, "Well you have a good time with the doctors. I'm going to find out what's really happening."

Joel sighed in exasperation. "We know what's really happening. It's obvious."

"Not to me," said Sara. "Look, I'm glad I met you. Now I know I'm not alone. But who knows how many other people are like us? Let's find out and do something about it."

Joel was glad that he'd met Sara too, but right now, she was being a pain. He didn't understand why she wouldn't accept the obvious fact that she needed help – medical help.

What he really should do is ignore her and go to the hospital. If she came with him, great - if not, it was her loss. Except... except deep down inside, he sort of agreed with her. Common sense told him that he must be the problem, but there was a little voice inside his head that begged to differ. He wished he knew how to silence that little voice, but now that it had an ally in Sara, it wouldn't be quiet.

He sighed again. "OK, how about this? We spend the rest of the afternoon investigating your suspicions, but if we don't find anything out by the time it starts to get dark, we go and see a doctor."

Sara gave Joel another quick smile. "Sounds good," she said. "Let's head over to the town center and see what we can learn."

CHAPTER SEVEN

In the cool, dark, cavernous room, steps were being implemented to address the problem.

CHAPTER EIGHT

Joel and Sara walked up the busy road towards town in silence. They passed the park where Joel's nightmare had begun in earnest, although now that he thought about it, perhaps the black hole in the fridge had really been the beginning. He had almost forgotten about this and the more he thought about it, the more he realized that it must be related to the rest of the day's events.

They took a left and headed over the bridge that crossed the train tracks to enter the town center. "Sara?" said Joel. "Apart from nobody knowing who you are, has anything else strange happened to you?"

"Like what?"

"You know... like suddenly coming across a black hole where there really shouldn't be one... like in a fridge or something?"

"Wow," said Sara. "Maybe you really are nuts."

"I'll take that as a 'no,'" said Joel, wishing he had kept the thought to himself.

They passed the short strip mall that included *FroYo's* and walked into the town center. It was a lively place with restaurants, stores, a movie theater, a nightclub and more, all crowded together on two streets – Main Street and Arch Lane. Main Street led straight through the town and out the other side, towards the hospital, police station and town hall. Arch Lane took the form of a semi-circle, beginning at the start of Main Street and rejoining it about quarter of a mile later, just after the movie theater.

The town was busy this Saturday lunchtime, filled with people going about their ordinary, everyday, mundane business. How Joel envied them. He wondered what Sara's plan of action was, or whether she even had one.

"We're going to start with the newspaper office," said Sara, as if she had read his mind. "Let's see if there have been any reports of anything unusual."

As far as Joel was aware, the town newspaper consisted largely of announcements about upcoming events, advertisements for local stores and stories about people who had done something special in the community. He couldn't remember ever seeing an actual 'news' story in its pages, but he didn't feel like arguing.

The newspaper office was located about half-way up Arch Lane, and as they made their way towards it, Joel noticed one of his friends walking towards them. Joel held his breath as the boy approached – perhaps this kid would recognize him and stop to chat for a few minutes. They could talk about the party they were at last week, their mutual friends who were no longer speaking to each other and the new activities that had been added at the rec center. Of course, no such thing happened. The boy walked right past Joel without even looking at him.

They reached the newspaper's offices and walked into the building. It had a small, but pristine lobby. In one corner, next to the large window, there was a low table with three chairs around it and a neat stack of newspapers on top. Facing the door was a long desk that stretched from one wall to the other, with a flap on one end that allowed people to pass through.

"Where is everybody?" said Sara. "I thought this place would be bustling."

Joel had to agree. Although he had never been to the newspaper's offices before, he had some vague idea that there would be people running around yelling "Stop the presses!" and "Hold the front page!"

Then again, perhaps not. Given what he had seen in the town's newspaper, an empty lobby was probably about right.

"Hello? Anybody here?" Sara's voice echoed in the lobby. "Hello?"

"Looks like we'll have to come back later," said Joel.

"We don't have time for that," replied Sara. "Follow me."

She walked over to the desk and lifted up the flap.

"I don't know," said Joel.

"Come on!" she urged. "You've only given me until tonight to figure this out, so you can't hold me up."

Joel was not at all sure that they should be wandering around the office without permission, but he didn't want to lose track of Sara. Shaking his head, he followed her to the other side of the desk. They walked over to a gray door that looked like it might lead to the newspaper's inner sanctum. Sara tried the handle, but it was locked. She jiggled it repeatedly, but to no avail.

"See?" said Joel. "They don't want us back there."

"Don't you find this a little strange?" asked Sara.

"Not really," said Joel. "It's a Saturday, so they're probably closed."

"So they leave the front door to the office unlocked when they're closed?"

"OK, perhaps they're out to lunch and forgot to lock the door."

"So they remember to lock this door," said Sara, jiggling the handle of the gray door once again, "but not the other one?"

"That seems perfectly reasonable to me," said Joel. He didn't know why she was making such a big deal about this.

"And you don't find it strange that apart from a pile of newspapers, there are no other signs of life here – no papers, pens, computers, coffee mugs, garbage – nothing?"

"They're probably just very tidy."

Sara groaned. "You really lack imagination."

"Or maybe you have too much," retorted Joel. "Look," he added quickly, hoping to avoid a full-blown fight, "we're not going to learn anything here. What now?"

Sara pushed past Joel and stormed out of the office. "And now my only friend is a drama queen," he muttered. "That's just great."

He walked round the desk and stepped out of the office into the midday sun. Sara was standing on the sidewalk with her arms folded, staring across the street. He was struck by how out of place she seemed in her brilliant blue dress. Everyone around her was wearing regular "daytime" clothes – shorts, jeans, sweats, T shirts and the like. Sara shone like a lone star in a dark night sky. Joel walked over to her.

"Shhh, I'm thinking," she said.

"I didn't say anything," said Joel.

"I know, but you were about to." She looked up and down the street. "We need to go somewhere we can watch people without arousing suspicion. Somewhere where lots of people will come and go, but nobody will pay any attention to us." She turned to face Joel. "You like coffee, right?"

Joel was not actually a big fan of coffee – he much preferred hot chocolate with whipped cream – but he decided to keep this to himself. "Sure."

"Great. Let's go to *Java One*. We can hang out there and see if anyone's acting strangely."

Java One was the most popular café in town. In addition to hot drinks, it sold a wide variety of delicious pastries and sandwiches and was a favorite place for people to hang out. "What exactly are we looking for?" said Joel.

"I'm not entirely sure," replied Sara. "People acting confused or lost – something like that maybe."

"And what are we going to do if we find someone who seems confused? We can't exactly go up to them and say 'Excuse me, but do you feel like you're going crazy because nobody seems to remember you?'"

"Why not?" asked Sara.

"Think about it. What would you do if someone walked up to you and said that?"

"I would say, 'That's exactly how I feel. How did you know?'" said Sara with a little smirk.

Joel sighed. "OK, but what if someone said this to you yesterday. What would you have done then?"

Sara shrugged. "I probably would have thought they're weird and said 'No.'"

Joel realized he was fighting a lost cause. "Fine," he said. "We'll do it your way."

CHAPTER NINE

Joel and Sara retraced their steps back towards the beginning of Arch Lane and took a right onto Main Street. *Java One* was a glass-fronted, two-story building, about halfway down the street, sandwiched between *Exclusive Attire* and *Petopia,* and it only took them a couple of minutes to reach it.

"You remember that I don't have any cash, right?" asked Joel as Sara opened the door.

"Ugh – no, I forgot," she replied, closing it again and running a hand through her hair. "And I lost my card sometime last night or this morning. I have no idea where it is."

"Great," said Joel. "Well, luckily I'm not hungry, but it's going to be awkward hanging out there without buying anything."

"It's not a problem," said Sara. "I do it all the time. We'll go straight upstairs to the lounge. Just follow me."

They walked into the store, and passed by the display cases, cash registers and the coffee bar without stopping. The air was warm and heavily scented with the aroma of coffee, which Joel had always enjoyed more than its actual taste. Next to the large window there were a few empty chairs and tables, but they ignored these and headed upstairs.

The lounge on the second floor of the café was given over to leatherette easy chairs and sofas, accompanied by small, round coffee tables. There were several ceiling fans that gave off a gentle breeze, and the walls were covered by customers' coffee-themed drawings and paintings. In the middle of the space there were also a few tables and chairs dedicated to a card game called 'Perfect Place,' which had always been a favorite of Joel's. He was actually rather good at the game and had won 80% of his matches. At least, that's what he thought he remembered... but perhaps this wasn't true – he had no way of being sure anymore.

The space was pretty full today. A dozen or so people, some alone and some with friends, occupied most of the sofas and armchairs dotted around the room, and there were a few different pairs playing Perfect Place. Joel and Sara walked over to a couple of empty seats next to the large window that faced the street and sat down.

"This is perfect," said Sara. "We can see everything that's going on outside and watch people more closely in here."

"I'm still not exactly sure what we are looking for," complained Joel.

"Neither am I," said Sara, "But I think we'll know it when we see it. Just keep your eyes open." She paused for a moment. "But try not to stare."

This seemed like very unhelpful advice to Joel. Watch everyone carefully, without looking at them too closely. He decided, however, to keep this opinion to himself and try to relax. In a few more hours, this adventure – or misadventure – would come to an end and he and Sara would get the help they needed: professional help.

As he sat there, Joel took in the scene around him. He noticed that he and Sara were not the only ones who hadn't purchased anything to eat and drink. Did that mean something? Probably not – Sara said that she used to hang out here without buying anything all the time. Come to think of it, when he came here to play Perfect Place, he usually didn't buy anything either. Unless of course, he had never been here before, because that was a lie like everything else he remembered. But that didn't make any sense. He knew what this lounge looked like before he walked into it a few minutes ago with Sara, so he must have been here before. And that must mean… actually, he had no idea what that meant, but he did have an idea.

"Sara, I think I'm going to play a quick game of Perfect Place."

Sara had been staring out of the window intently, looking for something out of the ordinary. "We're here to solve a mystery, not to play games."

"But if I go and play with someone, it will give me a chance to watch them more closely," said Joel. This wasn't actually his reason for wanting to play, but he thought it sounded plausible.

"Fine," said Sara. "But don't spend too long playing with one person. We're on a mission here."

Joel got up and walked over to a card table that was unoccupied. He sat down and waited for someone to come and challenge him to a game. His idea was very simple. If his memory of being a star at this game was real, then he would defeat almost everyone who challenged him. If, on the other hand, it was a lie, then he would probably be soundly beaten by most other players. To be honest, he wasn't entirely sure what he hoped the outcome would be, but at least he was taking some decisive action.

It only took a few moments for someone to walk over to the table. It was a tall, skinny guy – probably in his mid-twenties. Joel didn't recognize him, which was a relief given the way his day had been going.

"Want to play?" asked Joel.

"Sure," replied the man. "Prepare to lose."

Joel smiled. "We'll see."

The man sat down opposite him and looked down at the cards on the table. He reached to pick them up, but instead withdrew his hand quickly.

"Is everything OK?" Joel asked.

The man stood up and scratched his head. "I guess we can't play," he said. "Sorry." He walked over to another table that had opened up and sat down.

This seemed to be the sort of thing Sara was looking for –someone behaving oddly – and clearly deserved further investigation. Joel got up and walked over to the table where the man was now sitting. Just as he got there, a young woman stepped in front of him and sat down. She smiled at the man and blew him a kiss. He gave her a big grin in return

"Excuse me," said Joel, "But I was going to sit there." The man and the woman paid no attention to him and started playing. "Great," he muttered sarcastically. "Just ignore me – that's fine."

He walked back to Sara and slumped down in his chair.

"What happened over there?" she asked.

Joel briefly recounted the events at the card table as Sara watched the man and woman play. "Well, he seems perfectly normal now," she said, "But I agree that was strange. You want to try again?"

"Not with him, no," said Joel. "I'll go back and play someone else."

"OK, and I'll keep an eye on that guy to see if he does anything else unusual."

It took a few minutes for another card table to become available, but as soon as it did, Joel hurried over and sat down. He noticed that the man and woman from before were still playing their game, both intently focused on the cards and ignoring everyone around them. Joel understood entirely – he had always found Perfect Place to be utterly engrossing, which was one of the reasons he enjoyed it so much.

"Can I play?" Joel looked up and saw a girl with short blonde hair, dressed in jeans and a yellow tank top standing next to the empty chair. He guessed she was 11 or 12, but she could have been younger.

"Have a seat," he smiled.

The girl smiled back and sat down. She reached for the cards on the table, but stopped suddenly and pulled her arms back. "What's that?" she said. "What does it mean?"

Joel had no idea what she was talking about. "What does what mean?" he asked.

The girl didn't answer, but stared at the table for a moment. Joel followed her stare, but could see nothing unusual – just a regular brown, wooden tabletop with a deck of cards waiting to be used.

"Oh well, maybe we can play another time," said the girl as she stood up and started to leave.

"Wait!" called Joel. "Why are you leaving?"

The girl paid no attention and headed towards the stairs that lead to the ground floor.

"I said WAIT!" he yelled, jumping to his feet.

The lounge was immediately silent as if someone had hit the mute button. Joel had his back to most of the tables in the room, but was pretty sure that everyone was looking at him.

The girl turned and looked him in the eye. "Hey – it's rude to yell," she said, in a tone that reminded Joel of a parent talking to their child.

"Sorry, sorry, sorry," said Joel, desperately trying to recover the situation. "I just need to know why you stopped playing."

"Because we can't," said the girl. "Duh!"

Joel felt his anger start to rise again. "Look," he said, "I'm having a very bad day – the sort of day that you cannot even begin to imagine – and I'm just trying to understand what's going on."

"I don't think I like you," said the girl. "Goodbye." With that, she spun on her heels and walked down the stairs.

Joel could not believe this. Why was this girl walking out? It took all of his self-control not to chase after her, haul her back to the game table and force her to play.

He took a deep breath and turned back to face the room. Everybody had gone back to whatever they were doing, and nobody was paying any attention to him. Nobody, that is, except for Sara who was glaring at him in a less than friendly manner. He gave her a half wave and sheepish smile as a vague form of apology, and made his way back to where she was sitting.

"Way to keep yourself inconspicuous," said Sara as he sat down opposite her. "As far as I can tell, you are the only one who is acting weird in here. What was all that about?"

"It happened again," said Joel. "She sat down to play with me, and then suddenly changed her mind. All she said was 'We can't play.' It was just like the guy before."

"OK, let's think about this. Why would two perfect strangers sit down to play cards with you, and then suddenly change their minds and leave?"

"I'm not even sure they did change their minds," said Joel. "It was more like they *couldn't* play with me. At least, that's what they both said. It makes no sense."

"Well, we'll just add it to the list of things that make no sense today. What's that – number 75?"

Something about her tone bothered Joel. "You know, this isn't funny. This is my life we are discussing here, which just so happens to be falling apart."

"Our lives," corrected Sara.

"What?"

"This is our lives we are discussing – not just yours."

"Fine – our lives – but it's still not funny."

Sara leaned forward, putting her face within inches of Joel's. "So what would you like me to do? Run around, screaming and crying, waving my hands in the air? Is that what you want?" She sat back in her chair again.

"That's not what I mean, and you know it," said Joel. "It just feels like this is all a big, crazy puzzle to you. A puzzle you are having a great time trying to solve. If it were up to me, we would already be at the hospital talking to trained professionals who could actually help."

"Then go," said Sara. "Ignore what we discovered at the newspaper offices. Ignore what happened to you just now. Pretend *you* can explain everything by some form of bizarre memory loss or mental breakdown. Whatever works for you."

As far as Joel could recall, they hadn't learned anything at the newspaper offices, but she had a point about the card game. There was no way to explain what happened with the man and the girl, at least none that he could think of.

"Do you have a theory?" he asked her. "I mean, do you think you know what's going on?"

Sara sat further back in her chair and massaged her face with her hands. "I don't," she said. "When everything started going crazy last night, I thought I must be dreaming, but this is all much too real." She paused for a moment before continuing. "I do think that there's something big happening. Maybe we're nuts, maybe we're not, but either way, I think something is going on... something that I don't understand... something..." She trailed off into silence.

"Something what?" asked Joel.

She shivered. "I don't know – just, something."

CHAPTER TEN

In the cool, dark, cavernous room, the problem was being closely observed.

CHAPTER ELEVEN

They sat there in silence– Sara looking down at her lap, and Joel watching her. How he would love to be able to read her mind – to get inside her head and see for himself what was going on. Was she keeping something from him, either to protect herself or to protect him?

It occurred to Joel for the first time that perhaps he was foolish to trust her. He knew almost nothing about her and had just taken it for granted that everything she said was true.

"How old are you?" he asked suddenly.

Sara raised her eyebrows. "Too old for you."

"No, seriously. How old are you?"

"Fifteen," she replied. "How old are you?"

"Thirteen," said Joel. "How come I haven't seen you around before?"

"How would I know? It's a big town. I'm sure there are thousands of people you haven't seen – or have seen and forgotten."

"I'm pretty sure I wouldn't forget you," said Joel. He turned bright red. "What I mean is-"

"It's OK," interrupted Sara, flashing her ephemeral smile once again. "I'll take the compliment."

Joel could kick himself. How on earth had he let that slip out? He didn't even mean it the way she thought. Did he? The whole thing was insane. He needed to focus on getting back to normal as soon as possible, not whether or not he liked a girl. Anyway, he already had a girlfriend. Her name was... Wait, what was her name? Why was this so confusing? Of course - Cassandra! That was it! But she wasn't his girlfriend – he just had ambitions in that direction. So why did he think–

Sara interrupted his train of thought. "OK. Back to observation mode, and no more awkward banter."

They sat back in their comfy chairs, alternately looking out of the window and watching people in the lounge. Joel concentrated on the task at hand, rather than dwelling on his embarrassing blunder, but despite his best efforts he failed to spot anything out of the ordinary. People were going about their everyday lives as if this were just another normal day.

As he watched, Joel realized that he felt separate from these people. Their obvious normality, their simple routines, their contentment with life – all the things that Joel wanted for himself – made them seem like a different species. He remembered Coach saying "You do not belong here," earlier that day. At the time he had thought Coach was crazy, or at the very least had a seriously misplaced sense of humor, but now he felt the truth of that statement. Maybe Coach was right. Maybe he didn't belong here.

He wasn't sure how long he had been reflecting on this, when he heard a voice behind him. "Hey! How are you?"

Joel turned and looked up. A boy, actually more of a young man, was standing behind him. He was dressed like a basketball player – long purple shorts and a matching jersey with the number 16 on the front. His short blond spikey hair had a streak of purple running down the middle that matched his uniform, and his blue eyes were fixed on Sara. Joel was pretty sure he had never seen him before, but just in case he smiled and said "Hello."

The young man paid no attention to Joel. "I like your dress."

Sara looked up. "Thanks," she said. "I like your raccoon stripe."

The young man grinned. "Thanks. I'm Ryan."

"I'm Sara," said Sara.

"And I'm Joel," said Joel.

"Are you with him?" asked Ryan, pointing at Joel.

"No. Well, yes, but no. He's just a friend."

Joel tried not to feel insulted. Just a friend? Of course they were just friends, but there was something about the way she said it that stung.

"Cool," said Ryan. "Can I get you a coffee?"

Sara shrugged. "Sure," she said, "why not?"

"Great. Let's go."

Sara stood up to join Ryan.

"So you're leaving now?" asked Joel, feeling more than just a little miffed.

"I'll be back," said Sara. "Just keep your eyes open."

Ryan looked down at Joel. "Yeah kid," he smiled. "Just keep your eyes open."

The two of them headed downstairs leaving Joel sitting by the window. He couldn't believe this. What was Sara thinking? Here they were, their world falling apart, and she goes off with some random guy to get coffee. He wondered again why he had decided to put so much trust in this girl. If he had any sense, he would get up right now and head over to the hospital. He really didn't know what was keeping him here.

He sat there fuming for several minutes, thinking of all the reasons he should walk out of the café and leave Sara with her newfound friend. He barely noticed what was going on around him, not that there was much to see anyway.

Joel worked himself up into such a state thinking about how rude Sara had been to leave him like this, that he was almost ready to abandon her. He had just decided to get up and head downstairs when she reappeared and dropped down into the chair opposite.

"Here," she said, "putting a large cup of coffee and a Danish pastry down on the table. "These are for you."

"For me? How did you–?"

"I told Ryan that you were my little brother's friend and I was supposed to be looking after you. Then I mentioned how hungry you were and voila!"

Joel couldn't help but smile. "Was this your plan all along? That's so smart. Where is he now?"

Sara brushed a rogue strand of hair from her face. "I told him I had to get back to you. We're meeting tomorrow by the lake."

"You are?"

"Of course I'm not," said Sara, rolling her eyes. "But he was nice enough to buy us both a snack, so I had to say something."

Joel smiled again. He looked at the steaming cup of coffee and wished that he had told Sara that he preferred hot chocolate, but at least the Danish sounded good. He picked it up and was about to take a bite when a powerful wave of nausea washed over his body. His stomach clenched as if he had taken a low hard punch – the feeling was so intense he thought he would throw up right there.

Joel dropped the Danish and put his hands over his mouth in a desperate attempt to stop a volcano of vomit erupting. His head was pounding now, and he scrunched his eyes shut to block out the light.

Sara was watching him carefully. She didn't seem surprised by his actions, but nodded her head slowly. "Feeling sick? Head want to explode? Same thing happened to me."

Joel opened his eyes but didn't feel secure enough to speak yet.

"Luckily I did a better job of hiding it than you, so Ryan didn't notice. I was hoping it was just me, but I guess not." She sighed. "I wish I had some idea what's going on."

"Maybe the food is bad," suggested Joel, but even as he uttered the words, he realized that made no sense. Nobody else was sick and anyway, the pastry hadn't even touched his lips. "Never mind."

Sara seemed to be lost in her own world, gazing out of the window at the deep blue sky. She was completely still, reminding Joel of the first time he saw her. He wondered what she thought of him. Obviously, she liked him enough to get that guy to buy him something to eat, even if it did almost make him hurl. All of a sudden, he realized that Sara had shifted her attention and was now looking directly at him.

"I was just thinking how still you seem," she said.

"Weird," said Joel. "I was having the same thought about you."

Sara stood up. "Obviously, we have been sitting here too long. Let's get some fresh air."

"What happened to looking for people acting weirdly?" asked Joel, standing up with her.

"It's pretty clear that we're the only bizarre people in this café. Besides, I feel like I'm missing something — something that I should've figured out by now. Maybe a change of scenery will help."

As Joel and Sara walked towards the stairs, neither one noticed a tiny camera in the corner of the room follow their progress. But then again, they hadn't noticed that this same camera had been focused on them since they sat down, and they had no idea that a second camera picked them up now as they reached the ground floor and followed them as they exited *Java One*. As far as they were concerned, nobody was paying any attention to them. They were wrong... very wrong.

CHAPTER TWELVE

Joel and Sara stepped out into the early afternoon sun. If anything, Main Street was even busier than before and they pressed themselves up against *Java One's* window to keep from being swept up by the crowd.

"Follow me," said Joel, deciding to take charge at least for a few minutes. He set off in the direction of the movie theater which anchored the far end of the street. Sara fell into step beside him and the two of them walked through the throng of people in silence. Sara seemed to be lost in thought once again, so Joel amused himself by listening to snippets of chatter around him.

"But he didn't even like the dog."

"Well, whose turn is it now?"

"So I said, 'You don't know what you're talking about – cheese is the best.'"

"What's wrong with her?"

"I totally nailed it."

"Look at that girl."

"Let's head over to the arcade."

"How is she doing that?"

"OMG, what is up with her?"

"Don't touch her. She might be infected."

With a start, Joel realized that the last few speakers had been looking directly at him and Sara as they walked by.

"Sara?" he said in a low voice.

"I know," she replied. "We're suddenly the center of attention."

She was right – almost everyone who passed by was gawking at them now. Except that they weren't staring at both of them, just Sara. Joel stole a glance at her, but could see nothing different. She was still the same arresting girl in a blue dress that he had met a few hours ago.

"Is something wrong with the way I look?" asked Sara, as if she could read his mind.

"No – you look great," replied Joel.

"Thanks," said Sara, "but somehow I don't believe you."

People in front of them were moving to the edge of the sidewalk as she passed by, as if they were afraid to get too close. "Hey," called out a man's voice from the crowd, "That's not right. You should do something about that."

Sara came to an abrupt halt. "Why are you all staring at me?" she yelled at the group of people closest to her.

The crowd scattered, anxious to avoid a confrontation in the middle of Main Street, but Sara was not finished with them. "I said, 'WHY ARE YOU STARING AT ME?'" she bellowed after them.

Joel grabbed Sara by the arm. "Come on," he said, "let's get out of here."

Sara spun round and looked at him. "Why are they staring at me?" she growled.

"I honestly don't know," replied Joel. "You don't look any different than you have all day."

"What are you not telling me," she asked in the same quietly dangerous tone.

"Nothing," said Joel. "There's nothing wrong with the way you look. I have no idea what's going on, but we need to go right now." People were still staring at Sara as they walked past, and the looks she was getting were not friendly.

Sara nodded and with Joel still holding her arm, the two of them continued walking down the street. Sara kept her head down, avoiding eye contact with everyone. They had been walking in this manner for less than a minute, when Joel realized that people were no longer paying attention to them.

"Wait," he said to Sara.

She stopped, but did not look up. "What now?"

"Nobody's staring at you anymore."

She cast a furtive glance at the passing throng. "How come? What's changed?"

He looked back to where they had been standing before. "Well for one thing, we're not standing outside *Sensational Stationers* anymore. Maybe there's something about that store..." His voice trailed off as he realized he had no clue how he was going to finish that sentence.

"Something about it that made everyone act as if I was a mutant?" said Sara sarcastically, finally taking a good look around her.

"Everyone but me," said Joel. "You seemed totally normal to me. Well," he added, "Except when you started screaming at everyone."

"You're one to talk," chided Sara. "How old was that girl you were harassing in *Java One*? Anyway, I've been to *Sensational Stationers* hundreds of times – I love it there – and nothing like this ever happened before. Of course, this has been a day of many memorable firsts."

"Are you feeling brave?" asked Joel.

Sara eyed him suspiciously. "What do you have in mind?"

"An experiment," said Joel. "Let's retrace our steps and see if people start freaking out again."

"I don't know," said Sara. "I'm not sure I can go through that again."

"I'll be right by your side," said Joel. "And if things start to get crazy again, we'll run."

Sara shook her head doubtfully. Joel could see the anxiety written across her face, but something told him that he had to persevere.

"Look," he said. "You're the one who's been saying all along that we're not nuts, that there's something big going on. I've never agreed with you more than right now, and I want to figure it out."

Sara looked him straight in the eyes without blinking. "You're right," she said. "And by the way, I like you." Joel thought he was going to faint – she liked him! And then she ruined it. "You're a good kid."

"Thanks," said Joel, trying to keep the ocean of disappointment out of his voice. "I like you too."

There was her smile again. "I know you do." She smoothed down her dress. "OK, you're in charge, so lead on."

They walked slowly back towards *Sensational Stationers*. Nobody gave them a second look – they seemed like a couple of friends taking a pleasant stroll, enjoying the beautiful day. But if someone had been paying careful attention, they would notice anxiety and stress written large across the two of them. Sara was chewing on her lower lip and her arms were folded tightly across her chest. Joel was holding his arms rigidly at his sides and flicking his fingers rapidly, as if he was listening to a rock band playing in his head. They didn't look at each other and most of the time they kept their eyes firmly on the sidewalk, only occasionally glancing around to see if anyone was staring at them.

Joel held his breath as they reached the store. After waiting a moment, he looked over at Sara who was still keeping her head down. "You should probably look up," he said.

She gave the smallest of nods and slowly raised her head. Joel braced himself for an onslaught of catcalls and gasps from people passing by, but nothing happened. Nobody gave them a second glance."

Sara shrugged. "OK, so apparently *Sensational Stationers* does not turn me into a hideous monster."

Joel did not know how to respond. As far as he could tell, she had looked perfectly normal the entire time everyone had been staring at her. He wondered for a moment if it had been a group of people playing a prank, and on any other day this is probably the conclusion he would have reached, but not today. Today, it must mean something... but what?

"Let's get away from the crowd for a while," said Sara.

"I thought we were trying to watch people."

"I know, but I need to think. So much has happened, but all I have is questions. I need to start figuring out some answers."

This made sense to Joel, although he wished she had said *"We,"* instead of *"I."* He couldn't help but feel that Sara viewed him as less than her equal.

"Let's head over to the school," she continued. "It should be quiet there today."

The school complex consisted of three structures – the main building, where Joel had spent most of his time, the gymnasium and the science lab. All three had a contemporary design – smooth white concrete with elegantly rounded roofs – and were set in five acres of playing fields.

To reach the school, they had to walk back the way they had come – past *FroYo's* and over the bridge, away from the town center. From there, they took a left and walked close to a mile until they saw the trio of white concrete buildings. Nothing remarkable happened during the walk, which, when Joel thought about it, was actually quite remarkable.

They walked up a wide driveway that led to the main building – a white, circular structure with four floors. Instead of entering it, they walked past and headed over to a large playground to the left. As Sara had anticipated, it was deserted on this Saturday afternoon and they were completely alone.

They were not, however, unobserved. A tiny camera, hidden from view high above the central school building, had been following their movements from the moment they entered the grounds. It was part of the same network of cameras that had been watching them in *Java One* – a vast, secret grid that had prioritized Joel and Sara for surveillance.

Unaware of this intrusion into their privacy, Sara sat down on a swing. She wrapped her arms around the chains on either side of the seat and stared out at the cars driving by on the road. Joel sat down on the swing next to her and began to pump his legs, enjoying the back-and-forth motion.

"Having fun?" asked Sara.

"I'll take it where I can," said Joel.

Sara smiled. "I like your attitude, but we need to focus." She paused for a moment. "My boyfriend…" she paused again. "I mean the guy who I was dating…" she trailed off again and then shook her head in frustration. "What is wrong with me?" she said. "Why can't I remember his name? I'm sure I have a boyfriend. He's…"

"Is it Craig?" asked Joel.

"Yes!" Sara yelled with relief. "But how did you know?"

"You told me earlier – when we first met. Anyway, what about him?"

"He always used to say…" again, she came to a stop. "What is going on? I don't know what he used to say… I can't even think what he looks like! Why can't I remember anything about him?" She jumped off the swing angrily and stormed across the playground.

Joel thought back to a few hours ago when he had forgotten the name of… Whose name had it been? His girlfriend? No, she had been… Wait, did he have a girlfriend?

"Sara!" he called out to her. "Wait!"

She stopped in front of a large jungle gym and turned to face him. Her face was bright red and Joel wondered if she had been crying. "What?"

"I think this is another symptom of whatever is going on. Earlier today, I couldn't remember something about someone, and now I can't even remember who that someone was."

"Really?" said Sara. She wiped an arm across her eyes. "Are you just trying to make me feel better?"

Joel walked over to where she was standing. "I wish I was," he said, "But it's true. I didn't say anything to you because I didn't want to sound even more nuts."

Sara nodded. "It does sound nuts," she agreed.

"So come on then," said Joel. "It's time to turn all these questions into answers, right?"

"Right," said Sara, sitting down and leaning back against one of the metal bars in the jungle gym. "It's time for answers."

CHAPTER THIRTEEN

In the cool, dark, cavernous room, the problem was not being resolved as rapidly as anticipated. Additional measures were necessary.

CHAPTER FOURTEEN

"Do you think we're dead?" asked Sara.

Joel sat down on the ground next to her. "No. Why would you think that?"

"I don't know… things feel so unreal. Like this isn't real life. You know what I mean?"

Joel did know what she meant. When he reviewed the day's events, the word "unreal" summed things up very nicely, but he didn't think he was dead. While he had no personal experience with death as far as he was aware, he did not believe that this was what it would feel like. As a quick test, he pinched himself on the arm: good, he felt that. Dead people wouldn't feel a pinch, right?

"If we're dead," he said, "how come people can see us? How come we can open doors, sit down, stand up, walk, talk and everything else?"

"Can't dead people do those things?"

"If they could, wouldn't we see dead people everywhere?" asked Joel.

"Good point, although I've never known anyone who died," said Sara thoughtfully.

"Me neither," said Joel, "And I'd like to keep it that way."

"Then let's forget about death and think about what we know." Sara stretched her arms out in front of her and then rested them on her lap. "First: nobody we know recognizes us. Second: the newspaper office showed no sign of life—"

"I still don't see what's weird about that," interrupted Joel.

Sara ignored him. "Third: nobody can play Perfect Place with you at *Java One*. Fourth: trying to eat at *Java One* makes us violently ill. Fifth: a whole bunch of people on the street suddenly act as if I'm a mutant. Sixth: we're starting to forget things about our lives. Is that everything?"

Joel thought for a moment. "Number seven: neither one of us has any money."

"Right," said Sara. "So if we can just figure out what these seven things have in common–" She came to a sudden stop. "What was that?"

"What?"

She jumped to her feet, staring in the direction of the main school building. "Over there. Did you see anything?"

Joel looked over at the circular building but saw nothing amiss. "Nope – just the school."

As he uttered those words, the light in the schoolyard changed ever so slightly. It was nothing obvious, but it seemed to Joel that everything was a half-shade darker than a moment before. An eerie silence descended on the playground, as if someone had sucked the sound out of the air around them.

Before Joel had a chance to ponder these changes, three figures cloaked in pitch-black robes appeared around the curved wall. Their faces were as white as ghosts and the tops of their heads were covered in small craters, like the surface of a barren planet. The creatures were grotesque: they had bright red lips, large hooked noses, but no visible eyes. Each one was carrying a long black staff and at the end of each staff was a silver axe head.

"Oh no," he whispered. "No, it can't be... it can't be..."

These were the Henchmen – creatures who had only ever existed in his nightmares – but now they were here, at the school, no more than 50 yards from where he was standing.

In unison, all three started to walk towards him with slow, deliberate steps. Their mouths formed hideous grins and they began to make a soft moaning sound.

Joel was rooted to the spot. He couldn't move if he wanted to – these creatures were coming for him, just like in his nightmares, and there was nothing he could do to stop them.

Someone grabbed him by the arm and yanked him to his feet. It was Sara - tears were streaming down her face. "We have to run. We have to run."

Joel did not move. His feet felt like they were made of lead and he was incapable of any momentum. The Henchmen were closing in and soon they would have him.

Sara grabbed him by the shoulders. "Joel!" she screamed, "we have to run! Now!!"

Joel managed to tear his gaze away from the three approaching figures and look at Sara. He just couldn't make himself–

"Now!" she screamed again, pressing her forehead against his. She turned and sprinted towards the school gymnasium which was behind the main building. Joel shook his head quickly and ran after her.

They reached the large rectangular building and darted round the corner, out of sight of the creatures. Sara bent down, panting heavily and sobbing. Joel was in a similar state. He leaned against the concrete wall, gasping for breath. He couldn't believe that he had just sat there, waiting for The Henchmen to take him. "You saved my life," he wheezed. "You–"

"You have to look," interrupted Sara between breaths. "You have to see if it's gone."

Joel's stomach clenched at the thought, but he clearly owed her. He cautiously peered around the corner of the gym, praying that the creatures had disappeared. They had not. They were no more than 20 yards away now and moving more quickly. They had the same gruesome smiles and their axes glinted in the sunshine. Joel quickly ducked back around the corner.

"Still coming," he said, his voice trembling. "What now?"

"Keep running," said Sara. "Come on!"

They dashed along the outer wall of the gym until they reached the far end. Joel looked back and saw the three figures appear around the corner of the building and continue their relentless march towards him and Sara. He felt a rising sense of panic – there was no way to stop these monsters. They would keep on coming until they had him.

"The science lab," panted Sara. "Maybe we can find something in there to stop it."

Joel realized Sara was right. There had to be some chemicals or acids or something in there that would stop these creatures.

"Agreed," he said. "Let's go."

They ran faster than ever, driven by the fear of what was behind them and the hope that salvation was within their grasp. Joel reached the science lab first and pulled on the door. It was locked.

"Break a window!" yelled Sara as she came running up behind him.

Joel looked around. There was nothing to throw at the window. "With what?" he cried.

Sara pulled off one of her shoes and threw it at the nearest windowpane. It bounced off. Joel looked back towards the three Henchmen. They were moving even more rapidly and their moans had become deeper and more fearsome. He knew the end was near.

He took a step back, lowered his head and threw himself at the window. Sara screamed, but instead of slicing himself into a hundred pieces, Joel bounced back and landed on the ground.

"Wha–" Joel started to say, but he was interrupted by Sara.

"Don't let it get me!" she cried, pressing herself back against the door.

"I can't stop them!" yelled Joel.

Sara glanced over at him. "What do you mean them?"

"The three Henchmen!"

"You mean the giant spider?" said Sara looking back in the direction of their impending doom.

"There's no spider!" yelled Joel. "It's the Henchmen from my nightmares!"

"No, it's the giant spider from <u>my</u> nightmares!" Sara looked confused for a moment and then her whole body stiffened. "Oh God Joel... it's not real."

"What do you mean?"

Sara grabbed him by the shoulders for the second time in less than three minutes. "We're seeing different things! You're seeing something called Henchmen and I'm seeing a monstrous man-eating spider! They're not real – something tapped into our minds to find our worst fears."

Joel turned and looked at the three Henchmen. They were closer than ever and they seemed very real.

"You're not real!" screamed Sara. "You're not real!"

The Henchmen did not slow down. They would have Joel in a matter of seconds and then it would all be over.

"You're not real!" screamed Sara for a third time.

"You're not real!" Joel joined in. "You're not real!"

The creatures flickered.

"You're not real!!" the two of them screamed as one.

The creatures flickered again. And then they disappeared.

Sara sank to her knees, covered her head with her hands and started to sob. Joel watched her for a second, then slumped to the ground and gagged.

CHAPTER FIFTEEN

They sat there on the ground, bodies shaking as they gasped for air and sobbed. Joel's head was pounding and his body felt like it was on fire. For several minutes he was unable to formulate a coherent thought, but as his physical being started to relax, he tried to make sense of what just happened.

Sara was obviously right: those creatures were not real. But they weren't just any random creatures. They were swiped directly from his and Sara's worst nightmares. Did that mean that their own minds had betrayed them? Was this another symptom of the mental illness that he had suspected earlier in the day?

His ruminations were brought to an abrupt halt by the girl in the blue dress. "What do you want?!" she screamed at the sky. "Why are you doing this?"

The silence that followed her outburst was almost palpable. Joel looked around, but couldn't see anyone. "Who are you talking to?" he asked.

Sara continued to glare at the sky. "Them! It! Whoever or whatever is playing games with us!"

Joel reached out to touch Sara's arm, but she pulled away sharply. "What do you think you're doing?"

"I'm sorry," he said. "I was just trying to make you feel better."

"Well don't. Nothing is going to make me feel better, except this nightmare coming to an end." She wiped her eyes and stood up.

Joel did not feel quite ready to join her in an upright position, and remained on the ground. "You didn't see three men with axes?"

Sara was surveying the school grounds and didn't look down at Joel. "I already told you – what I saw was a giant spider, like the size of a car. It was terrifying."

"But it wasn't real," added Joel.

"No," said Sara. "Nothing's real... nothing."

Joel stood up. Sara had a vacant look in her eyes that he hadn't seen before and it worried him. "What are you thinking about?"

"Nothing is real, Joel, nothing."

"What do you mean?"

"Everything around us is a fake. We're being mocked."

"I'm real," said Joel, "And so are you."

"How do you know I'm real?" She turned and looked him directly in the eyes. "I mean really, how do you know?"

"I just know, OK?" said Joel. He reached out and touched the concrete wall next to him. "And this school is real."

Sara shook her head slowly. "That's just it," she said in a low voice. "I don't think it is." Joel couldn't imagine where this was going. "Let me ask you this," Sara continued. "How come we couldn't open this door?"

Joel shrugged. "It's locked, I guess. It's Saturday, you know."

"Then why couldn't we break the window?" asked Sara in the same quiet tone.

"I don't know. Maybe it's made of specially reinforced glass or something."

Sara walked over to the window. "Come over here. Take a look and tell me what you see inside the building."

Joel wasn't sure why they were wasting time with this, but after everything they had just been through, the last thing he wanted to do was aggravate his friend. He stepped over to the window and took a look. "OK. I don't see anything. So what? The lights are off. As I said, it's a Saturday."

"But you see nothing, right?" said Sara. "I mean absolutely nothing. No shadows, no shapes, nothing."

"Right," agreed Joel. "It's completely black."

"Think about this." Her voice was harder now, with a distinct note of irritation. "It's sunny outside. Shouldn't some of that sunshine make it through the window and light up the room – even a little bit? So how come it is pitch-black?"

Joel sighed – the conversation was spiraling towards yet another fight. He wished she didn't always overthink everything. "So maybe they have a shade that blocks out sunlight."

Sara stamped her foot in frustration. "Ugh! Are you totally incapable of critical thinking? Come with me."

She stormed off in the direction of the main building.

For a moment Joel considered letting her go. Why did she think she could hurl insults at him whenever she felt like it? Just because he disagreed with her, it didn't mean he was stupid. He had always tried to avoid stubborn, bossy people and now he was stuck with someone who fit both of those adjectives. And, of course, he <u>was</u> stuck with her. She was the only person who knew what he was going through and the only person who might be able to help. He had no choice but to follow her.

Well… that wasn't the only reason he was with Sara. Despite everything, or maybe because of everything, he liked her. Ugh, he really annoyed himself sometimes.

He caught up with her by the entrance to the main school building.

"Let's assume you're correct," she said. "Let's assume that the science lab is locked and that the window uses some super-secret technology that absorbs light."

"Like a curtain," muttered Joel under his breath.

Sara ignored him. "But this is the regular school building. We've been inside this place hundreds of times, right? There's no super-secret magic going on here." The sarcasm in her voice felt like a slap in the face to Joel.

"So," she continued, "Let's see if we can open the door. If the school is real, then we should be able to walk right in."

"Except it's a Saturday," said Joel who felt that Sara was missing a fundamental point.

"When have you ever known this door to be locked?"

The short answer was "never." As far as Joel could recall, this door was always open, but he wasn't sure if he had ever been here on a weekend. "Fine," he said. "Go for it."

Sara turned towards the door. She took a deep breath, grasped the handle and pulled.

It swung open.

Joel stepped past her and walked into the entrance hall. Everything was just as he remembered. On the opposite side of the room facing the main door was the grand staircase that led to the second and third floors of the building. It was an impressive structure: constructed from white marble, it was wide enough for a truck and adorned with elaborate, carved bannisters on both sides. Joel had always thought it seemed a little too extravagant for a school. Here on the ground floor, the auditorium could be found down a short corridor on the left, while a hallway on the right led to a series of classrooms.

He turned to face Sara who was still standing in the doorway. "Real enough for you?" he asked, failing to keep a touch of smugness out of his voice.

Sara walked in. "This doesn't prove anything," she said, and marched down the corridor to the auditorium. Joel followed, keeping his distance. She came to a set of double doors and pushed them open, revealing... the school auditorium.

"This doesn't make any sense," she said. "This shouldn't be here."

"What you mean," said Joel, a couple of feet behind her, "is that it doesn't make sense for your theory. Of course the auditorium should be here. It's always been here. The school is real, even if those monsters we saw weren't."

She turned to face him. "What about the science building?"

"Sara, it's a Saturday. Obviously they lock the door and pull the shades down on the weekend. That's all."

Sara did not look convinced, but for once she didn't argue. The two of them walked out of the school in silence, each consumed by their own thoughts. Joel was struck once again by how perfectly the word "unreal" described his day. It felt more like a plot of a melodramatic movie, than a day in the life of a 13 year-old boy. Phantom monsters, vanishing memories and lost lives were the stuff of fairytales, not real life.

Clearly, Sara had been thinking along similar lines. "Maybe the buildings are real, but the people aren't," she said as they walked slowly down the drive back towards the road. "Perhaps some alien force has replaced everyone in town with duplicates. Maybe they forgot about us somehow and now they are trying to make us go away."

This was probably the craziest idea that Sara had come up with all day, but as Joel wrapped his brain around it, he realized it sort of made sense. But it couldn't be true... could it? No, of course not. How could aliens have come and replaced everyone in the town? There's no such thing as aliens. And even if there were aliens, why would they waste their time on Joel's town? But it did explain a lot— particularly the weird way almost everyone was acting towards them. Did his family and friends not know him because they weren't really his family and friends? Did those people refuse to play Perfect Place with him because they didn't really know how to play the game?

"But what about the food?" he asked as they reached the main road. "Why weren't we able to eat anything?"

Sara pondered that question for a moment and then came to an abrupt stop. "Because it's alien food," she gasped, "and we are totally allergic to it. Oh my God, Joel, I think I've figured it out. I think this is what's happening." Her eyes shone with excitement.

"Wait," said Joel. "This cannot possibly be right. I agree that it would explain a lot – it really would – but are you seriously suggesting that we are surrounded by alien clones?"

Sara ran a hand through her hair. "I know," she said, "It's nuts, right? But think about it. It explains everything that's happened to us since last night."

"But if these alien clones want to get rid of us, why don't they just kill us or something? In fact, most people have been perfectly normal and nice to us."

His objection did nothing to dampen Sara's enthusiasm. "Excellent point. Let's go find out what they're thinking, shall we?"

Joel wasn't sure what Sara was planning, but had a feeling he wouldn't like it. "What do you mean?"

"I mean, let's go and talk to some people. We can tell them we know who they are and we want to know what's going on."

"You're not seriously suggesting we walk up to a stranger and say 'Excuse me, we think you're an alien clone who has replaced a human. What are you doing on our planet?' I don't think I can be part of that."

"You're right - we'll be subtle," said Sara. "We'll trick them into telling us the truth. If at first we don't succeed, we can talk to someone else."

Joel gave Sara a long hard look. The way she explained it, the theory almost sounded reasonable, but the idea that everyone was an alien clone was just insane. On the other hand, they had recently been chased by imaginary monsters so perhaps an alien invasion wasn't all that farfetched.

Sara ignored his stare. "I think it's best if we avoid crowds and try to find people who are alone. I just can't decide if it would be better to interrogate someone we know or someone we don't."

"Interrogate?"

"Sorry – you know what I mean."

Joel really hoped he didn't.

"Anyway, what do you think – a friend or stranger?" asked Sara.

Joel thought for a moment. "Perhaps a friend: we would know a lot about them, so it should be easier to trick them into telling us what's going on."

"OK, friend it is. Let's see…" Sara's voice trailed off. She shut her eyes tightly and furrowed her brow.

"Sara?"

"I can't think of anyone," she whispered.

"OK, well–"

"No," she interrupted, opening her eyes and looking at Joel. "I mean I can't remember anyone – not my friends, not my family, nobody. They're all gone."

CHAPTER SIXTEEN

Sara took several deep breaths and looked up at the sky.

"It's OK, it's OK," Joel tried to soothe her.

A lone tear appeared in the corner of her right eye and started to make its way slowly down her face. It took all of Joel's self-control not to reach out and wipe it away.

"This means I don't know who I am anymore," she said. "I don't know anything about myself."

"I know who you are," said Joel softly. "You're Sara. You're super smart and funny and pretty and sometimes a bit yelly."

Sara rewarded his kindness with the smallest of smiles and wiped her eyes with the back of her hand. "You're sweet, Joel, but it doesn't change what's happened to me. I've forgotten everything."

"Do you remember me?" asked Joel.

"Yes," said Sara thoughtfully, "I remember everything from today." She paused for a moment. "I also remember places like the park, the town center, different shops and things like that. I just don't remember anything about my life. I know I had trouble trying to think about my boyfriend earlier, but I didn't realize I had forgotten everything."

"Wait," said Joel, "How come you know you have a boyfriend?"

"Because you and I talked about him in the playground... I can remember talking to you about Craig, but I can't actually remember him. That's so bizarre."

"Says the girl who was chased by a giant, man-eating spider."

Another fleeting smile. "What about you?" she asked. "Can you remember anything about your life?"

Joel was silent for a moment. He knew the answer to her question, but didn't want to admit it. As long as he didn't say anything out loud, perhaps it wouldn't be true. But it was no use pretending: Joel remembered nothing. His life had gone missing, and he was afraid he would never get it back.

"No," he said quietly, "I can't remember anything."

"I'm sorry," said Sara as she reached out and gave his arm a gentle squeeze.

Joel swallowed hard and gave a small nod in response.

"But do you remember telling me about your mom and dad this morning? And your friends Ben and Cassandra?"

"I do," said Joel slowly, "and you're right – that is SO weird. How can I remember *telling* you about them, but not actually remember them?"

"I don't know," said Sara, "But it's time we got some of our questions answered. Let's go."

She strode off purposefully, heading back in the direction of the town center. Joel walked by her side. He watched the cars streaming by on the road. "So do you think that these cars are being driven by alien clones?"

Sara gave him a suspicious glance, unsure if he was trying to be funny.

"No really," said Joel. "Do you think *everyone* has been replaced? And what do you think the aliens have done with all the people?"

"I know how ludicrous it all sounds," said Sara, increasing her pace slightly, "But it is the only theory we have right now. Unless you have a better idea...?"

Joel wished he did. He was still not comfortable with the notion of an alien takeover – it was just too fantastical – but he had no alternative explanation to offer. Nothing he could think of would make sense of what they had experienced today.

"Well then," said Sara, "let's find someone to interrogate."

Joel wished she would stop using that word.

"Remember, we're looking for someone who is alone. We don't want to make things harder than they need to be."

Joel gave her a quick glance. "You said we would be subtle, right?"

"Right," agreed Sara. "Subtle."

After a few minutes they reached the street that led to the town center. They had just crossed the bridge when Sara pointed to someone sitting by themselves on a pale-yellow bench outside *FroYo's*.

"Our first victim," she said, slowing down to a stroll as they approached the young woman. "I'm just kidding!" she added, when she saw the look of alarm on Joel's face.

Conveniently, the woman was sitting all the way on one end of the bench, leaving more than enough room for Sara and Joel to sit down next to her. She ignored their arrival and continued to eat her giant frozen yogurt. At a guess, Joel would say it was a chocolate vanilla combination with sprinkles, cookie crumbs and jelly beans.

"Hi!" said Sara.

The woman looked over at them. "Hello," she smiled. "Nice afternoon."

"It is," said Sara. "Perfect weather."

The woman nodded but said nothing.

"Are you new around here?" asked Sara. "I don't remember seeing you around."

"I've been here for a few months."

"Nice," said Sara. "Where are you from?"

The woman gave her a strange look. "You know I can't say. Anyway, I don't think it's any of your business."

"Sorry," said Sara, "I didn't mean to be rude. My name's Sara, by the way, and this is my friend Joel."

The woman smiled. "I'm Caroline. This is good yogurt."

"*FroYo's* is the best," chimed in Joel. "I really like the 'FroYo Six.' Have you ever tried–?"

"So," interrupted Sara, trying to keep the conversation on track, "do you come here a lot?"

"No," said Caroline. "Not a lot, but I needed something to eat, so thought I would try this place. It's good to try different things."

"It is," Sara agreed. "Do you have a lot of friends?

Caroline finished her snack and stood up. "You ask a lot of strange questions. Do you want to be my friend? Is that why you're asking?"

Sara was taken aback by the question and was unsure how to respond.

"Well it's not going to happen," continued Caroline. "I can't be friends with you." She turned and started to walk towards the town center.

"Hang on!" called Sara. "Why can't we be friends? What's wrong with me?"

The woman did not look back. "I don't know, but there's something. Sorry."

Sara turned to Joel. "Did you hear that?" she asked excitedly. "That was totally weird, right? I really think we're on to something."

"Me too," agreed Joel. "Something about that woman was way off. But the problem is, she didn't admit to anything and I'm not sure how we're ever going to find out what we need to know."

"We have to keep trying," said Sara. "I don't know how long we've got."

Joel did not like the sound of that. He hugged his knees to his chest and looked directly at his friend. "What do you mean you're not sure how long we've got?"

"Think about it," said Sara. "Doesn't everything seem to be getting worse? At first people didn't recognize us, then we started to forget things, then we couldn't eat, then crazy monsters attacked us and now we have no memories of anything."

Joel hadn't thought about this, but now that Sara said it, he realized she was right. "What do you think is going to happen next?"

"Nothing good."

Joel shivered, despite the warmth of the afternoon sun. "Then we'd better find someone else to talk to," he said. "How about this guy?"

As they watched, a teenage boy walked out of *Mario's Pizzeria*.

"Excuse me," Sara called out as he passed them. "Can we talk to you for a minute?"

The boy looked at Sara and smiled. "Sure. That would be epic!" He walked over to the bench and sat down next to her. Joel guessed that the boy was probably sixteen or seventeen. He had dark hair, dark sunglasses and a hint of a goatee. For some reason Joel took an instant dislike to him.

"I'm Ethan," he said, still smiling at Sara. "Can I buy you a *FroYo*?"

Joel sighed inwardly. Once again, some boy was going to flirt with Sara and act as if Joel didn't exist. He knew this was all part of the plan, he just didn't like it.

"No thanks," she replied. "I'm not hungry."

Ethan shrugged. "OK," he said. "Why's a beautiful girl like you hanging out at *FroYo's* on a Saturday afternoon?"

"Just relaxing," said Sara.

"Cool." Ethan stared at her for several seconds. Just when it was about to become uncomfortable, he spoke again. "How come we haven't met before? Is this your first time?"

"No," said Sara. "I've been here for a long time. How about you?"

"Almost a year," he said. "I like it here. It's a fun place."

"It is," agreed Sara.

It is not, thought Joel.

"Where are you from?" she asked.

Unlike the woman before, Ethan had no problem answering her question. "Pittsburgh," he said, "In Pennsylvania. How about you?"

"I'm from here," she replied, hoping that was true.

Ethan laughed. "Funny. I like you." He leaned forward and looked around Sara in the direction of Joel. "Hi," he said.

Joel gave a weak smile in response. "Hello."

"I'm Ethan," said Ethan.

"I know: I heard. I'm Joel."

Ethan leaned back again and turned to Sara. "Want to be friends?" he asked.

"Yes," said Sara enthusiastically. "I would love to!"

"Great!" said Ethan. Then he frowned. "Oh, never mind. Maybe some other time, right?"

"What's wrong with now?" asked Sara.

"Who knows?" said Ethan, shrugging again.

"What?" interrupted Joel, with more than a touch of frustration in his voice. "That doesn't even make sense."

Ethan leaned forward again so that he could make eye contact with Joel. "Look dude, it's not my problem, OK? There's no need to get all excited."

"Yes," said Sara glaring at Joel. "Just calm down."

Joel couldn't believe it. Sara was siding with goatee boy? She was supposed to be on his side.

She turned her attention back to Ethan. "So, I guess you're not allowed to be my friend? Is that it?"

"I suppose so," said Ethan. "I'm sure everything will be OK soon though, and then we can be friends."

"I see," said Sara thoughtfully. "When do you think that will happen?"

Ethan grinned. "Wow, you're keen." Joel really didn't like this boy. "I don't know… whenever you're OK again. Hopefully soon – I definitely like you."

"Thanks. Where are you headed?"

"To the arcade." Ethan stood up. "Wanna come?"

"Maybe later," Sara replied. "What's at the arcade?"

Ethan gave her a funny look. "Video games, of course. Haven't you ever been there?"

"Of course, of course," said Sara. "I just wondered if there was anything special there at the moment."

Ethan shrugged. "I don't think so – as far as I know, they never change the games."

Joel was delighted that the boy seemed to be leaving. He didn't want to spend another minute with Ethan or his goatee. He wondered for a moment whether he had always been this harsh about other people, or whether Sara brought it out in him.

"So, will I see you there later?" asked Ethan.

Sara smiled. "I think so."

"Epic," said Ethan. "Bye for now." He strolled off in the direction of the town center.

"I didn't like him," said Joel, as soon as Ethan was out of earshot.

"Of course you didn't," said Sara. "If it makes you feel any better, I wasn't a big fan either. But that was weird again, right? The way he said 'Let's be friends,' and then, 'Oh, we can't be friends – I'm not allowed.'"

"It reminded me a bit of trying to play Perfect Place at *Java One*," said Joel. "People saying they can't play with me – not they won't play or they don't want to play – but they *can't* play."

"You're right," agreed Sara. "It's definitely the same sort of thing. There's a force at work here... something that is trying to control us. The whole 'Alien' theory is making more and more sense to me. Maybe they haven't just taken over the town. Maybe it's the whole world."

While Joel recognized that Sara's idea about aliens explained a lot, there was something about this theory that continued to trouble him. "But if these people were all aliens, why would they want to make friends, or try to play games with us? It doesn't make sense."

"You're right again," said Sara. She tapped her fingers on her knees as she considered the problem. Joel noticed that her nail polish was perfect – pretty remarkable, given the day they were having. It was a luminescent pale blue with flecks of silver and it complemented her dress perfectly.

"Maybe they don't realize we are different until they are really close to us or spend some time with us, or something like that," said Sara.

"Maybe…" said Joel. "But I'm not sure what we're learning by talking to them, apart from the fact that everyone is acting weirdly, and I already knew that."

"Well, we have to do something," said Sara. "Eventually, one of them is bound to slip up and reveal something to us."

As they were talking, a tall man dressed in a dark blue suit and red tie crossed the bridge and walked towards them. He looked almost shiny, as if someone had given him a thorough polish before he set out that morning.

"Shall we try again?" asked Sara, nodding in the direction of the man.

"Sure, why not?" said Joel.

"Why don't you do the talking this time," Sara suggested. "Maybe you'll have more success than me."

Joel was not sure how he was going to approach the conversation, but had no time to consider his options. The man walked directly over to where they were sitting and stood over them, a little closer than Joel would have liked. He smiled. "Joel. Sara. Please come with me. Now."

CHAPTER SEVENTEEN

In the cool, dark, cavernous room, there was an increasing sense of urgency. The problem was causing ripples in the environment - new tactics were required.

CHAPTER EIGHTEEN

Joel couldn't believe his ears. This man knew his name. This man knew Sara's name. He desperately tried to remember whether he had met him before, but just couldn't recall anything specific prior to today.

The man took a step back. "Joel and Sara. Please come with me. Now." His voice was flat and entirely lacking in expression.

"Who are you and how do you know us?" As usual, Sara got straight to the point.

The man stared at her. "That is not important now. Please come with me."

"It might not be important to you, but it is very important to us," said Sara.

"Right," added Joel, feeling he should contribute something to the conversation.

The man turned his attention to Joel. "I am here to help. Come with me and I will help you." The man had dark, intense eyes – almost completely black – and Joel felt himself withering under their scrutiny.

"I'm not sure I believe you," said Sara.

"I am here to help," the man repeated. "Please come with me."

Sara stood up. Just a few inches separated her from the man. "You're not real," she said. "You're not real." She repeated the mantra several more times before he interrupted.

"I am real. I am here to help. Come with me." He turned and walked in the direction of a dark blue van that had pulled up at the side of the road.

Joel looked up at Sara. "I don't trust him," he said. "I don't think we should follow him and I definitely don't think we should get in that van."

"Me neither," said Sara, "But this is big. Something is trying to make contact and we need to investigate."

"Need to?" said Joel.

"Yes – need to. Come on." She started to walk towards the van.

Joel got to his feet. "Sara," he said. She stopped and looked back at him. "We have to be careful – really careful. This feels dangerous." With those words, he walked over to her and the two of them slowly made their way to where the man was standing by the van.

As they approached, the man stretched his face into a cold smile. "I am here to help," he said once again. "Come with me." He slid open the door to the van. "Step inside."

The inside of the van looked dark. Actually, it wasn't just dark, it was pitch-black. There was no light, no shadows, no murky outlines – just impossible blackness. It was just like the fridge this morning – a black hole of emptiness.

They were only a few feet from the van now and the man stepped to one side to let them in.

"Sara," whispered Joel coming to a halt and grabbing her arm, "I'm not getting in the van. Look at it."

"I know it seems creepy," she said, "but I think we need to take a look."

"It's not just creepy. It's a void. If we get in there, I think we'll disappear forever."

Sara turned and looked at him. "We have to figure out what's happening here, and this might be our only chance."

"No," said Joel. The determination in his voice came as a surprise even to him. "I'm not getting in there and neither are you. It's suicide. There has to be another way."

Sara withdrew her arm from his grip. "OK, then what do we do?"

The man had been observing this interaction, steadily smiling, but saying nothing until now. "You must come with me," he declared in his monotone voice. "I will help you."

"Tell us who you are!" demanded Joel.

The man took a step towards them. "You will learn everything if you come with me."

As if by magic, another man, dressed identically to the first, appeared from the other side of the van. "We are your friends," he smiled.

Joel and Sara started to back away.

"Joel, did you notice that when those monsters tried to get us we were all alone?" asked Sara.

He didn't respond – his attention was firmly fixed on the two men.

"And now these guys are trying to make us go with them, and we're alone again."

Joel took a quick look around him. Sara was right. There was nobody else in sight.

"So," she continued, "I think we should find a crowd."

Joel glanced at Sara. "I vote for running."

The two of them turned and sprinted in the direction of the town center. They didn't look back and didn't stop until they reached the junction of Main Street and Arch Lane. All around them, life carried on as if it were just another perfectly ordinary day – people were shopping, chatting, laughing, flirting, playing. Nobody was paying any attention to their plight.

"We've been doing way too much of this today," panted Sara.

Joel couldn't agree more. He looked all around him, but there was no sign of the two men or the van.

"Those two men," said Sara, "was it just me, or were they twins?"

"I don't know if they were twins," said Joel, "But they looked a lot alike. And they dressed the same way too. Do you think they were real?"

Sara thought for a moment. "Well, we both saw the same thing, right? Two men, tall, black hair, dark eyes, dressed in a suit and tie?"

Joel nodded.

"Then I'm guessing they were real: freaky, but real."

"And they didn't disappear when you yelled at them," added Joel, "So I bet you're right. But if they were real, then what were they?"

"I think they were the aliens, or the aliens' representatives or something like that. I don't think they were human."

Joel knew what she meant. They hadn't seemed like real people. "What about the inside of that van? It was like a black hole. It almost makes me wonder..." his voice trailed off as he noticed the expression of pure terror on Sara's face. She was staring up Arch Lane, lips parted, eyes wide and unblinking. Joel turned to see what she was looking at.

It took a few seconds for his brain to process the information his eyes were feeding him: one of the men from the van was standing about ten yards away, staring directly at them with the same fixed smile on his face.

It felt like the earth shifted under Joel's feet and he staggered backwards, bumping into Sara. She put her arm on his shoulder to steady him.

"It's, it's…" he stuttered.

"I know," Sara whispered. "How did he get there?"

Joel fought to keep his panic under control. "I have no idea… maybe he drove and we didn't notice him?"

Sara shook her head. "There's no way we wouldn't have seen that van pass us."

"Then what are you suggesting?"

"I suggest we get lost in the crowd."

That sounded like a good idea, but Joel was rooted to the spot. It was the same feeling he had had when he first saw the Henchmen at the school – he wanted to move, but his body seemed to have shut down.

Sara gave him a shove. "I said, let's go."

They turned from the man and pushed their way into the throng of people who were milling about on Main Street. As they slowly made their way along the sidewalk Joel looked back, but there was no sign of anyone following them.

CHAPTER NINETEEN

Blaring music, flashing lights and hordes of people. Yes, thought Joel, this was definitely a good place to hide.

Club Mode was dominated by a large, circular dance floor in its center. A giant disco ball spun slowly above, lit up by a myriad of red, blue and white spotlights. There were chairs and sofas dotted around the edge of the dance floor, and a bar that served snacks and beverages on the far wall.

Sara and Joel walked about halfway round the dance floor until they found a free sofa.

They sat down and for a few blissful minutes found themselves distracted by the spectacle before them. Dozens of people were dancing their hearts out – moonwalking, hustling, twisting and doing the centipede – the whole scene was mesmerizing. But this was not the only thing vying for Joel's attention. Sara was sitting closer to him than usual. Her proximity made his skin feel warm and tingly. He wondered how she would react if he casually reached out and took her hand in his. No, no – not now. He had to concentrate on their problems, not sit and daydream.

He stole another glance at her and wondered what was going through her mind as she stared at the dancers. Did she ever think about him? Good grief, he was doing it again!

Thankfully, Sara interrupted his train of thought. "What do you think those two men wanted?"

"I don't know," replied Joel, "But that van would've been the end of us. I'm sure of it. It was a dark, empty void and I think it would have swallowed us whole."

"OK, so let's assume they wanted to remove us somehow. Why would they wait until now? What's different now?"

Joel shook his head. "I have no idea. This whole thing is craziness heaped on top of insanity."

"Well, I'll tell you one thing that was different," said Sara. "They were trying to be friendly." She could see the look of incredulity on Joel's face. "No, hear me out. Instead of sending monsters, having people yell at us on the street or wiping our memories, they tried to be nice."

"Nice?" Joel could barely believe what he was hearing.

"Yes. What was it they kept saying? They were our friends. They were here to help."

"That's what made them so creepy," said Joel.

"I know, but I don't think they realized that. I think they were trying to be friendly." Sara ran her hand through her hair.

"Well, they need more practice."

"Exactly," said Sara. "They don't really know *how* to be friendly. They've observed people being friendly to each other, and this is their imitation of it."

"Sara..." said Joel.

"Think about it. They've tried to scare us and that didn't work, so now—"

"Sara!" This time the urgency in Joel's voice got her attention. "Over there," he said. "By the door."

Sara looked across the mass of people on the dance floor and saw what had alarmed her friend. It was one of the men from the van. He was standing perfectly straight, completely motionless, and he was smiling at them.

Almost in a trance, Joel raised a hand and gave him a small wave. The man waved back.

"What are you doing?" demanded Sara.

"I don't know," he replied uncertainly. "Just being friendly, I guess."

"Well, stop it."

Joel turned to face Sara. "How could he have found us here? We weren't followed – we kept checking."

"We must have missed him. We need to get out of here without him seeing and I know a way."

"There's no other exit," said Joel. "We're trapped unless we can make him move from the door."

Sara grabbed his hand. "No other exit that you know about," she said. "Come on." She jumped to her feet, pulling Joel up with her. He was in no mood to resist, and besides, she was holding his hand, so that was something.

Sara walked quickly towards the refreshment bar with Joel in tow. As they reached the counter, she veered to the right and firmly pushed the wall. Joel heard a swishing sound, and the wall slid open. Before he had time to express his astonishment, they were walking down a steep flight of stairs that ended in a brightly-lit passageway. The walls and ceiling were painted white and the floor seemed to be made of concrete.

Joel ran his fingers along the smooth walls. He had no idea that this place existed and wondered how Sara had discovered it. "Ummm..." he began.

"I found this a long time ago," said Sara. "It was when…" her voice trailed off. Joel didn't need to ask why — he knew she couldn't remember.

Sara shook her head in frustration. "Come on — there's no time to lose." They hurried down the passageway. Joel looked over his shoulder, but as far as he could tell they weren't being followed.

"Where does this lead?" he asked.

"It comes out at the back of the gazebo in the town green."

The town green was located on Main Street, just beyond the movie theater. It was too small to be called a park, and its only distinctive feature was a bright red gazebo at one end. Talent shows and other live events occasionally took place there, but mostly, it was a place where people relaxed in the sunshine.

"Then what?" said Joel. "We can't just hide in the gazebo."

"We head back to the town center and try to get lost in the crowd again."

Joel had some serious doubts about this plan. That man had been able to locate them in *Club Mode* without any difficulty.

Before he had time to dwell on this concern, they reached a ladder at the end of the passage. Sara climbed up, followed by Joel who was careful to keep his eyes down. When she reached the top, she opened a hatch and stepped up into the gazebo. The sun was getting lower in the sky now, and she shielded her eyes from the glare as Joel joined her.

The gazebo had a narrow bench that ran around three quarters of the structure. Somebody was sitting on the far side, but they didn't seem at all perturbed by Joel and Sara's sudden appearance. Of course, because the sun was in his eyes, Joel couldn't see them very well.

As Joel closed the hatch, the person stood up and took a step towards them. "Please come with me," he said in a familiar, expressionless voice. "I am here to help you."

It was one of the men again. The sound of the voice sent shivers down Joel's spine. How had he got here before them? It just wasn't possible. And then it dawned on Joel – there really was no way to escape. These men would find them wherever they ran, wherever they hid.

Joel turned and looked at Sara. She was standing by the hatch, seemingly frozen in place. Her arms hung at her sides and her mouth was slightly open as if she were about to say something. If it weren't for the tears streaming down her face, she could have been mistaken for a statue.

Joel put a hand to his own face and discovered that his cheeks were wet with tears too. He hadn't even realized he was crying.

The man took another step towards them. "I am your friend," he said. "You do not belong here. I will take you where you belong."

Joel looked at Sara again and then did something he had never done before. Something he had never known anyone else to do. Something that was totally and absolutely against the rules. He took a step towards the man and punched him as hard as he could in the jaw.

The man staggered backwards and landed on the bench with a thump. Joel turned to Sara who had closed her lips and was now staring at him instead of the man.

"Run!" he yelled.

She didn't move but continued to stare at him. Joel wasn't sure if it was fear, confusion or surprise that he saw in her eyes. Perhaps it was a combination of the three.

He walked back to her quickly. To his horror, she flinched as he approached. Did she think he was going to hit her? He would never do that! "Sara…" he whispered.

She took a deep breath and wiped her arm across her eyes. "OK," she nodded, "Run." With that, she darted past Joel and jumped off the gazebo.

Joel took another look at the man. He was sitting, unmoving, with his eyes closed. He didn't seem too badly hurt – there was no blood or anything – so perhaps he was OK. Or not… As Joel watched, the man started to fade. He became more and more transparent until Joel could actually see the bench and gazebo through him.

Joel dug the heels of his palms into his eyes and rubbed vigorously. He must be imagining things – perhaps the direct sunlight had hurt his vision? He stopped rubbing and took another look.

The man was sitting there as if nothing had happened. He wasn't transparent, not even a little bit. As Joel wondered whether he was losing his last ounce of sanity, the man's eyes opened. He didn't look at Joel, however, but just stared into the distance, not blinking and not moving.

Joel had no interest in finding out what might happen next. He took a running jump off the gazebo and sprinted away in search of Sara.

It took him just a few seconds to reach the end of the town green. His heart was racing as he looked around, but not because of physical exertion. Sara was nowhere to be seen. A hundred fears flooded Joel's brain. What if she had been taken by the other man? What if she had disappeared into the van? How would he ever find her? What if he never saw her again?

He remembered the way she flinched when he had approached her in the gazebo. Was she afraid of him just because he hit someone? Was she hiding from him now? That would be ridiculous.

Joel looked back at the gazebo. Nobody was there. He didn't know whether to be relieved that the man was well enough to walk away or alarmed that he had no idea where he had gone.

He looked up and down the road again. If he headed in one direction, he would end up at the police station and hospital. There was no way that Sara would have gone there. He turned the other way and started to run back towards the movie theater and town center. He had to find Sara and make sure she was safe. Nothing else mattered.

CHAPTER TWENTY

Sara didn't stop running until she reached the movie theater. She paused for a moment at the imposing red-brick building, trying to catch her breath. She felt exhausted – more tired than she had ever been in her life – but she couldn't stop here. Sara looked around her and decided to get lost in the crowds on Arch Lane.

Her mind was spinning, unable to process the events of the past few minutes. How had that man been waiting for them in the gazebo? It was like witchcraft. And... Joel had hit him.

She had never seen anyone throw a punch. It was forbidden. It was unthinkable. It would never be tolerated. And she was pretty certain he had done it for her.

She looked over her shoulder for Joel, but there was no sign of him. He was probably trying to find her, but she couldn't let him succeed. Joel was dangerous now. He must have lost his mind, which was pretty reasonable under the circumstances, but still... he hit someone. She wondered if the man was dead. She wondered if she wanted the man to be dead.

Sara considered what she knew about Joel. Really, very little. It was amazing she had ever trusted him. But there was something special about Joel, something she recognized the moment she met him, something reassuring. And her instincts had been correct. Joel had been there for her from that first moment. He was definitely on her side.

But now that had ended. The thought saddened her a little and annoyed her a lot. He had ruined everything by hitting that man. Now she was alone with no one to turn to and no one to confide in. But if she was honest, it wasn't just the idea of being alone that upset her.

She liked Joel – genuinely. He was nice and kind and sometimes funny. True, at times he could be maddening, but then so could anyone.

Anyway, it didn't matter anymore. Joel wouldn't last more than five minutes after what had happened. He was probably gone already. She stopped dead in her tracks. That was a strange thought. What did she mean, *He was probably gone already*? Gone where?

Perhaps she meant the police would have arrested him already? No… that wasn't it. She shook her head in frustration – her memory must be failing her again.

Sara resumed walking up Arch Lane, casually glancing in the different storefronts that she passed by as she pondered her situation. She really had no idea what her next move should be. She was being pursued by two freaky men, had no friends, couldn't remember anything about her life and had no money. But she was a survivor. Whoever or whatever had been torturing her all day had not defeated her. As long as she could hang on and avoid capture, at some point they would have to change their tactics and negotiate.

She suddenly realized that there had been something amiss with the last two or three storefronts she had passed. The windows had been blurry, making it impossible to see what was inside, and there had been no doors. She kept on walking and realized that more than half of the stores on the street were like this.

Sara stopped at the next blurry window she came to and pressed her nose against the glass, trying to see what was on the other side. It was impossible to see anything. The window didn't even feel like real glass – it was sort of plastic and hard.

She looked around at the crowds of people walking up and down the sidewalk. Nobody was paying any attention to the fake storefronts. It was like they didn't even notice anything was wrong.

Sara racked her brain trying to remember the names of the stores that used to be in these spaces, but her memory failed her yet again. It was time for an experiment.

"Excuse me," she said to a young woman with bright red hair who was walking past her, "what's the name of this store?"

"I don't know," the woman replied, without stopping.

Sara tried the same question on ten more people. On four occasions she got the same response. Another five people totally ignored her, but the last one – a teenage girl who she guessed was about the same age as Joel – stopped.

"It's nothing, right?" she said.

Sara stared at her for a moment before responding. "Right…"

"Right then," said the girl, and walked off.

Sara watched her saunter away and wondered if she should follow. She seemed to know more than most people around here and might be useful.

She turned back to look at the window again and let out an audible gasp. The man was back. The man from the van, the man from *Club Mode*, the man from the gazebo. He was leaning against the storefront staring at her and he wasn't smiling anymore.

Sara steeled herself. She was shocked to see him, but she was not going to be intimidated by this thug anymore. Obviously, he couldn't hurt her or he would have done so already. He was nothing.

She took a step towards him. "What do you want?" she snarled.

The man did not reply, but continued to gaze at her with his dark, impassive eyes.

"Well whatever it is, you're not going to get it." Sara turned her back to the man and was about to walk away when she changed her mind. She spun around, ready to tell him how ridiculous he was, how she wasn't scared of him and how *she* was going to be watching *him* from now on, but he was gone.

Vanished.

She looked around, trying to spot him in the crowd, but he was nowhere to be seen.

Sara felt a momentary surge of power. She had scared the man away. She was invincible. Before she could really enjoy the feeling, however, she became aware that several people had stopped on the sidewalk and were gawking at her.

"That's not right," said a young man to a woman standing next to him.

"It's weird," agreed the woman.

"What's weird?" demanded Sara. "What are you staring at?"

The crowd was growing larger as more people stopped to look at her. Sara looked down at herself. She seemed perfectly normal – her arms, her legs, her dress, her shoes – nothing seemed wrong. She ran her hands through her hair and felt the contours of her face. Normal. It was all normal.

"She should be removed," said another voice from the crowd.

"Maybe we should help her," said a tall blonde woman who had just joined the group. "She looks stuck."

"I wouldn't do that," said a man who seemed to be with her. "You don't want it to happen to you."

This was more than Sara could handle. "WHAT ARE YOU TALKING ABOUT?"

A ripple ran through the crowd. A couple of the bystanders walked away, but most just stayed, waiting to see what would happen next.

"Sara!"

It was Joel. He pushed through the middle of the throng and grabbed her by the hand. She looked at him in disbelief. "How did you find me?"

"Large crowd of people... voices yelling and screaming... it wasn't difficult."

Sara knew he was trying to be funny, but she was not in the mood and pulled her hand away from his. "It's happening again," she said. "Just like before."

"I know," said Joel. "And now I know why. We need to get away from these people – from everyone. Come on."

CHAPTER TWENTY-ONE

In the cool, dark, cavernous room, all measures had failed. But it no longer mattered. The end was coming.

CHAPTER TWENTY-TWO

Sara and Joel turned away from the crowd and walked quickly up Arch Lane. At first a few people stopped and stared as they passed by, but before long nobody was paying them any attention once again.

"Well?" said Sara.

Joel ignored the question. "Why did you run away?"

"You hit someone, Joel. You can't do that. Ever. Come to think of it, how come you're still here? You should be gone."

Joel shook his head. "I have no idea. But you didn't have to run off like that. I would never hit you."

"I know."

"I don't even know what made me do it," continued Joel. "It was like something snapped inside me."

They reached the end of the road and took a left on Main Street, away from the town center.

"I just can't believe you're still here," said Sara.

"Yeah, that's what I've heard all day," said Joel. "'You don't belong here.'"

Sara stopped suddenly and grabbed Joel's arm, her eyes ablaze with excitement. "That's it," she said. "We don't belong here. That's what this is all about."

"What do you mean?" asked Joel.

"Listen. We've been going around thinking that aliens or something have taken over our town, but what if we're the aliens and this isn't our town?"

They had reached *FroYo's* and sat down on the bench where they had talked to the woman and boy earlier that day. "I'm not an alien," said Joel. "And this is our town."

"What do you remember about your life here?" asked Sara.

Joel slumped back and put his hands in his pockets. "Nothing. You know that."

"Maybe that's because we don't have a life here to remember. Maybe we really do belong somewhere else."

"I don't mean to be rude," said Joel, "but this is like the tenth theory you've had today."

"Wow, thanks," said Sara sarcastically. "All I've been trying to do is figure things out."

Joel looked at his friend. "Sorry," he said. "But I know something you don't."

"What?"

"The people all pointing and yelling at you – remember?"

"Of course I remember," said Sara.

Joel swallowed hard. He did not think that Sara would like what he had to say. He sat up straight, took his hands out of his pockets and rubbed his temples.

"Well?" Sara demanded.

"You flickered."

She stared at him for a moment, trying to understand what he had said. "I flickered?"

"You know – like a light going on and off really quickly. You flickered."

Sara ran a hand through her hair and stood up. "I don't understand," she said. "What do you mean?"

Joel remained seated and looked up at her. "You disappeared for a split-second and then reappeared again. I saw it happen three or four times, but it must have been going on for a while before I got there."

"Don't be stupid," she said hoarsely. "You just blinked."

"I've been blinking my whole life. I've never seen anyone flicker before."

"Well I've never seen anyone punch somebody before," retorted Sara.

Joel was silent for a moment. "Fair enough – now you have. And now I've seen someone flicker."

Sara sat down again, leaned forward and put her head in her hands. Joel wondered if she was going to yell at him, but she just stayed like that, not moving and not making a sound.

"Are you OK?" he asked.

Sara did not reply.

Joel put his hand on her back and started to rub gently. She didn't move, but he could hear her breathing.

"Did you feel anything?" Joel said.

"When?" murmured Sara.

"When you were flickering."

She didn't respond. Joel continued to rub her back for a few more seconds, but stopped when she sat bolt upright.

"Obviously, I didn't flicker," she said decisively. "There must be something wrong with your eyes."

"And the eyes of everyone else who was staring at you?" said Joel. "I can't explain it, but I know what I saw."

"I didn't flicker!" Sara exclaimed with even more force. "You must have imagined it, or everyone imagined it or something! I didn't disappear and then reappear! I'm not a magician!"

Joel said nothing as he watched a car drive over the bridge, heading away from the town center. It was red – his favorite.

"Joel, are you even listening to me?"

"I'm listening, I just don't know what to say," he said softly.

"Maybe it was a trick of the light."

Joel shook his head but remained quiet, judging that anything he said right now would only make Sara angrier. He had been so relieved when he had found her, but the relief had turned to fear a second later as he watched her flicker repeatedly. He just wasn't sure how much more of this nightmare he could stand.

"And I suppose you think that this is what happened to me earlier today, when everybody was staring at me outside *Sensational Stationers*? Why didn't you see it then?"

Joel shrugged.

Sara was about to point out another obvious flaw with his observation, when she saw it.

"Joel..." she said slowly.

"Sara, I know you don't want to hear this, but–"

"Joel!"

Something about her tone made Joel's entire body tense up. "What?"

Sara was staring at him. "You... you're..." she stuttered. "You're flickering."

Joel patted himself down – arms, legs, body... everything seemed to be where it was supposed to be. "Am I doing it now?"

Sara shook her head. "No. You stopped." She stared at him for a moment. "It's true? Oh my God, it's true..."

Joel didn't say a word. Ever since he had seen her flicker, he had been expecting this. He felt strangely calm and remote about the whole thing, as if it was happening to someone else and he was merely observing the situation. Perhaps it was... maybe he was watching a really good movie and had become so engrossed in the plot that he imagined himself to be the main character. But, of course, that was not the case. He was definitely the star of this tale – well, the co-star at least...

"What are you thinking about?" asked Sara. "You looked like you were a million miles away, and I could have sworn you were smiling. That's not exactly the reaction I expected."

"Sorry," said Joel. "I was imagining we were movie stars."

Sara raised her eyebrows. "OK..."

Joel sighed. He looked around, but there was no sign of the two men or the blue van. Apparently, the punch had been effective. He turned his attention to Sara. She was as radiant as the moment he first saw her, despite everything they had been through. For a moment, he wished that he had put on something a little nicer than shorts and a T-shirt that morning, but really this was the least of his problems. He was brought sharply back to reality by seeing Sara flicker again. "So what now?" he asked.

Sara was quiet for a few seconds. She shook her head slowly and then looked up at Joel. "Nothing."

"What do you mean, 'nothing'? You always know what to do. You always have a plan." As he uttered those words he realized how true they were. He had come to rely on Sara and couldn't imagine how he would have coped without her by his side. Her theories, her passion and her conviction had kept him strong even in the darkest moments.

"Not this time," said Sara in a quiet voice. She was silent again. Joel sat back down next to her and gave her a playful push. "Come on…"

"I think this is all coming to an end," she continued. "I mean, *we* are coming to an end."

Joel didn't like the sound of that. It made him feel squirmy inside. "Don't talk like that. We've been through worse than this."

Sara flickered again. "I don't think so Joel. I think this is the end of our time here." She turned and looked him directly in the eyes. "All day long things have been getting worse and worse, and now we are fading. It's like the curtain coming down on a horrible play."

"I was thinking more of a movie," said Joel.

Sara gave a weak smile. "Whatever. We're disappearing. You were right from the beginning. It's not everyone else, it's us. "

"I wasn't right – I thought we were sick or something," said Joel. "We're not sick."

"No… we're not sick. I just don't think we're real."

"That's crazy talk! I'm real and you're real."

"I mean, we're not real to this place." Sara ran her hands through her hair and massaged the back of her neck. "It's all so obvious to me now, and I don't know why it took me so long to figure out. It's why nobody knows us, it's why we have no money, it's why we can't eat, it's why we have no memories. We don't belong here. We're not real here. And now we're disappearing."

Joel felt a rising sense of panic. "There must be something we can do," he said. His voice sounded whiny, even to him. "We can't just give up!"

"There's a difference between giving up and knowing when there's nothing else to be done," said Sara.

"What if we find those two men and agree to go with them? Maybe they really can help us!"

"Do you see those men anywhere?" asked Sara. "I guess that whoever sent them doesn't care anymore, now that we're disappearing."

Joel could not fathom this change in his friend. She was the strong one. She was the fighter. She was the one who didn't give up. What happened to her? She flickered again and Joel wondered how many times he had done the same thing during this conversation. "So, we just sit here until we disappear?"

Sara stood up and smoothed her dress down. "It'll be dark soon," she said. "Let's go somewhere with a view."

She reached down and took Joel's hand in hers. He stood up and the two of them walked away, hand in hand, leaving *FroYo's Frozen Yogurt Emporium, Mario's Pizza* and the town center behind.

CHAPTER TWENTY-THREE

Sara and Joel sat on the grass at the top of Aulvirt Hill overlooking North End Park. The sun had set, but they could see the streetlights below and a steady stream of car headlights making their way along the road. It all seemed so idyllic, serene and beyond their reach.

Sara leaned her head on Joel's shoulder and closed her eyes. Despite everything that had happened to them that day, he felt content. Sure, he was scared too – he had no idea what would happen next – but he was grateful to have Sara by his side. He put his arm around her shoulder and she leaned in more closely.

"Are you frightened?" she asked in a quiet voice.

"A little," he said. "How about you?"

"A little," she agreed. "But I feel better having you here."

She flickered for a moment.

"What do you think is going to happen to us?" asked Joel.

"I don't know. What happens when someone who isn't real disappears? Maybe we become real? That would be nice."

"You're real to me," said Joel. "You're probably the most real person I ever met. So if you are going to tell me that you're not real and everyone else is, then I say reality is for losers."

Sara smiled. "What do *you* think is going to happen?"

Joel closed his eyes for a moment. "Something awesome," he lied. "Something so awesome, I can't even imagine it."

They sat in silence, staring at the lights below. Occasionally, Sara or Joel would flicker but otherwise they were still.

"I wish I understood more," said Sara after a few minutes. "I think it would be a relief just to know what was going on. Just to know who I am, what I am doing here and why I am disappearing. That would be good."

Joel didn't respond immediately, but as he sat there a story began to form in his mind. "Well," he said slowly, "this is what I think. I think we are in heaven. I mean, not exactly heaven, but maybe a place you wait before you go to heaven. I think this place was made to look like the town we came from, just to make us feel better, and now we are moving on to the real heaven." He was quiet for a moment. "That's what I think."

Sara smiled again. "That is beautiful. You really are awesome Joel. I know I haven't always been super-nice to you today, but I liked you from the moment we met. A lot."

Joel sighed, but it was not a sigh filled with sadness and regret. It was a relaxed, content sigh. How weird was that? Here he was, slowly disappearing from the world, but feeling more at ease and comfortable than at any time he could remember.

He made a decision. An important decision.

"Sara," he said. "I've never said this to anyone before, because I've never really meant it. But I feel like I should say it to you."

No, wait, that wasn't right.

"I mean, I *want* to say it to you. Really. Because I mean it. So here goes. I think that—"

A cool breeze brushed his cheeks and she was gone. His shoulder was still warm from where her head had been resting, but she was no longer there. Her smile, her wit, her energy, her intellect, her warmth — all gone.

Joel was alone. The streetlights still shone, cars still sped along the road below, the town continued to bustle with activity, but Joel was alone. He was too drained to cry and too exhausted to be scared. He really didn't care how much longer he had. It didn't matter anymore. In fact, if it was up to him, he—

CHAPTER TWENTY-FOUR

In the cool, dark, cavernous room, a door opened. A light came on and two men wearing white lab coats strode into the space. They looked around at the rows and rows of computers and made their way to a screen located on the far wall.

"So this is the main server room that controls the virtual world and game?" asked the taller of the men. He had silver-gray hair tied back in a ponytail and wore steel-rimmed glasses on his nose. "I've never been in here before."

"Normally there's no need to," said the other, "except for routine maintenance and occasional upgrades. The game usually runs itself without any problems." He was carrying a small tablet computer and reviewing some data on the screen as they walked.

"So what happened?" inquired the man with the ponytail.

"I'm not exactly sure. There was some sort of glitch that caused a major bug in the virtual world. Usually these things are fixed immediately, but this one was stubborn."

They reached the screen, and the shorter man put his tablet down on a desk. Unlike his colleague, he was almost completely bald and a little overweight. "Let's take a look," he said. He touched the display and it sprung to life. A virtual keyboard appeared at the bottom of the screen and the man began typing a series of commands.

"Doesn't the game get bugs all the time?" asked the taller man. "I mean, what's the big deal?"

"The big deal is that the game was almost unable to fix the problem." He stared at the screen for a moment and then pointed at some code. "See – here. The artificial intelligence function in hundreds of players' avatars went wrong. Their accounts were all shut down and the avatars deleted, but two of the avatars didn't delete. They basically continued in the game without a player. That's unheard of.

"The game launched several new security procedures to try to remove the two rogue avatars, but nothing worked. They actually carried on living in the virtual environment, without any user control, almost like real people. They interacted with other players' avatars and with computer-generated characters. There was nothing the game could do about it."

"I never liked the idea of the avatars having artificial intelligence," said the taller man. "There's something fundamentally wrong about it — we give them a backstory, emotions and the ability to interact with the virtual world even when the users are not controlling them. It's like we're playing God."

"Yes, yes," said the other, "But they only do this within the limits set by the game and the player. I know we call it artificial intelligence, but the avatars don't *really* think for themselves. In reality, they're behaving according to a set of rules set by the player and the game."

"But these two were thinking for themselves?"

"I know it seems that way, but obviously they couldn't actually do that. It was just some software code that had gone wrong, that's all."

The taller man took off his glasses and massaged the bridge of his nose. "What were their names?"

"Whose names?"

"The two avatars — the ones that were thinking for themselves."

The shorter man consulted the screen again. "Let me see," he said swiping through pages and pages of data. "T639OG46E — avatar name Sara, and T28HE14R4 — avatar name Joel."

The taller man replaced the glasses on his nose. "What happened to them at the end?"

"Eventually, after almost 24 hours, the game was able to delete them. But you have to understand, this usually takes less than a second – it was almost like the avatars were fighting back."

"Do you think Joel and Sara knew what was happening to them? Do you think they were scared at the end?"

The shorter man scratched his head. "You're talking as if they were real, intelligent, independent people. They weren't – they were avatars in a game. Nothing more."

His colleague frowned. "Really? Avatars that made decisions by themselves, lived within the virtual world with no user or game control, survived for almost 24 hours and actively resisted deletion... they sound like intelligent, independent people to me." With that, he turned and started to walk away.

"I want a full description of all of their movements from the moment the game lost control of them to the moment they were deleted," he said over his shoulder. "By tomorrow morning. Then we'll have a conversation about just how intelligent and independent they were."

The shorter man sighed – it was going to be a long night. He picked up his tablet computer and followed his colleague out of the room. As he reached the door, he switched off the light.

The cool, dark, cavernous room returned to a state of calm.

Flicker